Reproductive Rights

Other Books in the Global Viewpoints Series

Anti-Semitism and the Boycott, Divestment,
    and Sanctions Movement
Chemical and Biological Warfare
Citizenship in the 21st Century
Climate Change and Population Displacement
Collective Guilt: Slavery, the Holocaust,
    and Other Atrocities
The Food Chain: Regulation, Inspection, and Supply
Gender Diversity in Government
Islam in Society
Life After Death? Inheritance, Burial
    Practices, and Family Heirlooms
The Rise of Authoritarianism
Violence Against Women

GLOBALVIEWPOINTS

Reproductive Rights

Kathryn Roberts, Book Editor

GREENHAVEN
PUBLISHING

Published in 2020 by Greenhaven Publishing, LLC
353 3rd Avenue, Suite 255, New York, NY 10010

Cover image: GIANLUIGI GUERCIA/AFP/Getty Images
Map: frees/Shutterstock.com

Library of Congress Cataloging-in-Publication Data

Names: Roberts, Kathryn, 1990- compiling editor.
Title: Reproductive rights / Kathryn Roberts, book editor.
Description: First edition. | New York : Greenhaven Publishing, [2020] |
  Series: Global viewpoints | Audience: Grades 9 to 12. | Includes
  bibliographical references and index.
Identifiers: LCCN 2018059178| ISBN 9781534505605 (library bound) | ISBN
  9781534505612 (pbk.)
Subjects: LCSH: Reproductive rights—Juvenile literature. | Human
  reproduction—Law and legislation—Juvenile literature. | Birth
  control—Law and legislation—Juvenile literature. | Women›s
  rights—Juvenile literature.
Classification: LCC HQ766 .R44475 2020 | DDC 323.3/4—dc23
LC record available at https://lccn.loc.gov/2018059178

Manufactured in the United States of America

Website: http://greenhavenpublishing.com

Contents

Foreword **11**

Introduction **14**

Chapter 1: Reproductive Rights Around the World

1. In the **United States** *Roe v. Wade* Changed Everything **19**
   Savanna Fox

   In 1969, a young woman in Texas wanted to end her pregnancy. Known as Jane Roe, her attorneys challenged the laws that made abortion illegal, and in 1973, that case was presented to the Supreme Court, becoming what is now known as the case of *Roe v. Wade.*

2. In the **United States** Before *Roe v. Wade* Abortions **25**
   Were Life-Threatening
   Marie Solis and Jo Baxter

   This is the story of Jo Baxter, who found herself pregnant at age twenty in 1965 when abortion was illegal. Baxter shares her story of the decision to end her pregnancy, the process, and gives insight into what could happen if abortion protections are removed in the present day.

3. In **Ireland** Citizens Vote "Yes" to Legalize Abortion **30**
   in Landslide Referendum
   James Hitchings-Hales

   In 2018, the Republic of Ireland voted with 66.4 percent in favor to repeal a clause to its constitution that restricted abortion rights. Prior to the referendum, abortion was illegal in all cases, including cases of rape, incest, or abnormality of the fetus.

4. In **Latin America** Women Are Punished for Their **35**
   Abortions
   Verónica Osorio Calderón and Kristof Decoster

   Between 2010 and 2014, 95 percent of abortions in Latin America were performed in unsafe and unsanitary conditions, as only four countries in Latin America allow abortions.

5. In **South Korea** a Half-Century-Year-Old Abortion   **40**
Ban Needs Another Look

Kelly Kasulis

In 1953, South Korea banned abortions, making them
punishable by up to a year in prison or a fine of up to two
million won. In 2018, that ban is being challenged, with a
South Korean doctor claiming that the ban places danger
on women's health.

Periodical and Internet Sources Bibliography   **47**

Chapter 2: Societal Impressions of Reproductive Rights

1. In the **United States** the Supreme Court's Hobby   **50**
Lobby Ruling Allows Companies Exemption
from Providing Contraceptives

Mary Agnes Carey

In 2014, the Supreme Court voted 5-4 to allow a key
exemption in health care law, ruling that for-profit
businesses could assert religious objection to the Obama
administration's contraceptive mandate.

2. The Misconceptions About Planned Parenthood   **56**
Are Intentional

Dayna Evans

With one in five women visiting a Planned Parenthood
in her lifetime, this viewpoint details the reasons why—
many of which do not include seeking an abortion. The
misconceptions about Planned Parenthood can long be
traced to the assault against women's rights to safe access to
reproductive health.

3. In the **United States** Maternal Mortality Is   **62**
Shockingly High

Nina Martin and Renee Montagne

In 2011, Lauren Bloomstein died shortly after giving birth
at the age of thirty-three. Her death sheds light on the rate
of maternal mortality in the United States, where the rates
are highest in the developed world.

4. American Men Have No Reproductive Rights   72
   Michael Bargo Jr.
   While much of the focus on reproductive rights is centered
   on a woman's access to reproductive care and the right to
   choose, there are few laws at either the state or federal level
   that make any effort to protect men's reproductive rights.

5. Reproductive Coercion Is a Form of Sexual Assault   77
   Kat Stoeffel
   Stories of women discovering that their birth control has
   been sabotaged are more common than people think, even
   more common than the story of the stereotypical gold
   digger lying about being on birth control.

Periodical and Internet Sources Bibliography   82

Chapter 3: Reproductive Rights and Religion

1. In the **United States** Crisis Pregnancy Centers   85
   Are Challenging the Reproductive FACT Act
   Linley Sanders
   Crisis Pregnancy Centers, which do not want to inform
   women about low-cost public programs for family
   planning, are challenging California state law AB 775,
   which mandates that all California reproductive health
   centers provide this information.

2. In **Islamic Countries** Family Planning Programs   90
   Help Strengthen Overall Development
   *Babar Tasneem Shaikh, Syed Khurram Azmat, and
   Arslan Mazhar*
   One of the many roadblocks to family planning services
   in the Middle East, specifically Pakistan, is religion. In
   the more rural areas, a lack of access also has a significant
   impact on a woman's access to these services.

3. Conflict Between Religious Beliefs and Pediatric Care   102
   *Armand H. Matheny Antommaria, MD, PhD, FAAP
   and Kathryn L. Weisem, MD, MA*
   The relationship between religion and medicine is
   complex, and there are many people who use religion as
   a reason to refuse medical treatment for their children.
   Religious exemption has also led to child abuse and neglect

and the funding of alternative spiritual healing practices
that are popular but unproven.

4. In the **United States** Parents Refuse Medical Care **111**
for Children in the Name of Christ
Jason Wilson
States like Idaho have laws that shield people from
prosecution, even in crimes of child neglect and abuse,
even manslaughter, courtesy of the veil of religious
exemption. These laws have led to the deaths of a large
number of children who did not receive proper medical
care, as their parents chose unproven alternative methods
of faith-based healing.

Periodical and Internet Sources Bibliography **120**

Chapter 4: The Importance of Having Access to Reproductive Care Around the World

1. Countries Around the World Beat the US on **123**
Paid Parental Leave
Jessica Deahl
Of the 193 countries that make up the United Nations,
only a handful do not have laws in place to protect paid
parental leave: New Guinea, Suriname, a few nations in the
South Pacific, and the United States.

2. In **East Africa** and **Southern Africa** HIV and AIDS **129**
Hit Hardest
Avert.org
In 2016, South Africa accounted for one-third of the region's
new HIV infections, while another 50 percent occurred in
eight other countries, including Mozambique, Kenya, Zambia,
Tanzania, Uganda, Zimbabwe, Malawi, and Ethiopia.

3. In **France** Expansion of Access to Reproductive **139**
Health Services Should Pave the Way for Women
Around the World to Control Their Own Bodies
Rebecca Brown
In 2014, France became the latest country to affirm a
woman's right to an abortion and also took measures to
address gender inequality in the country.

4. In the **United States** the Unintended Teen Pregnancy   **145**
   Rate Is Among the Highest in Developing Nations
   Emily Bridges
   While teen pregnancy has declined since its peak in 1990,
   the United States still has one of the highest rates of teen
   pregnancies than many industrialized nations because
   of a lack of reproductive education and access to family
   planning services,

5. Sexuality and Reproductive Health After Giving Birth   **154**
   Family Planning NSW
   Reproductive education does not end with getting
   pregnant. It is important to educate woman on the changes
   a body undergoes following birth and how to safely recover
   from pregnancy.

6. Inequalities Stand in the Way of Achieving   **159**
   Reproductive Rights
   Bjorn Andersson
   When women are able to plan for the timing and size of
   their families, they are able to complete their education
   and contribute to the economy via entering the workforce,
   which improves conditions in their countries overall. But
   because of a number of inequalities this has been difficult
   to achieve.

Periodical and Internet Sources Bibliography   **163**

For Further Discussion   **165**

Organizations to Contact   **167**

Bibliography of Books   **172**

Index   **173**

Foreword

"*The problems of all of humanity can
only be solved by all of humanity.*"
—Swiss author Friedrich Dürrenmatt

Global interdependence has become an undeniable reality. Mass media and technology have increased worldwide access to information and created a society of global citizens. Understanding and navigating this global community is a challenge, requiring a high degree of information literacy and a new level of learning sophistication.

Building on the success of its flagship series, Opposing Viewpoints, Greenhaven Publishing has created the Global Viewpoints series to examine a broad range of current, often controversial topics of worldwide importance from a variety of international perspectives. Providing students and other readers with the information they need to explore global connections and think critically about worldwide implications, each Global Viewpoints volume offers a panoramic view of a topic of widespread significance.

Drugs, famine, immigration—a broad, international treatment is essential to do justice to social, environmental, health, and political issues such as these. Junior high, high school, and early college students, as well as general readers, can all use Global Viewpoints anthologies to discern the complexities relating to each issue. Readers will be able to examine unique national perspectives while, at the same time, appreciating the interconnectedness that global priorities bring to all nations and cultures.

Material in each volume is selected from a diverse range of sources, including journals, magazines, newspapers, nonfiction books, speeches, government documents, pamphlets, organization newsletters, and position papers. Global Viewpoints is truly global, with material drawn primarily from international sources available in English and secondarily from U.S. sources with extensive international coverage.

Features of each volume in the Global Viewpoints series include:

- An **annotated table of contents** that provides a brief summary of each essay in the volume, including the name of the country or area covered in the essay.

- An **introduction** specific to the volume topic.

- A world map to help readers locate the countries or areas covered in the essays.

- For each viewpoint, an **introduction** that contains notes about the author and source of the viewpoint explains why material from the specific country is being presented, summarizes the main points of the viewpoint, and offers three **guided reading questions** to aid in understanding and comprehension.

- **For further discussion** questions that promote critical thinking by asking the reader to compare and contrast aspects of the viewpoints or draw conclusions about perspectives and arguments.

- A worldwide list of **organizations to contact** for readers seeking additional information.

- A **periodical bibliography** for each chapter and a **bibliography of books** on the volume topic to aid in further research.

- A comprehensive **subject index** to offer access to people, places, events, and subjects cited in the text.

Global Viewpoints is designed for a broad spectrum of readers who want to learn more about current events, history, political science, government, international relations, economics, environmental science, world cultures, and sociology— students doing research for class assignments or debates, teachers and faculty seeking to supplement course materials, and others wanting to understand current issues better. By presenting how people in various countries perceive the root causes, current consequences, and proposed solutions to worldwide challenges, Global Viewpoints volumes offer readers opportunities to enhance their global awareness and their knowledge of cultures worldwide.

Introduction

> *"Unless we reduce inequalities in women's reproductive health and rights, the world will fail to achieve the UN's Sustainable Development Goals that underpin the 2030 Sustainable Development Agenda, and the most important goal, poverty reduction—SDG 1 —will be blocked. When women are able to control their fertility, including by avoiding early marriage or unintended pregnancy, they can finish their education, enter the paid labour force and gain more economic power."[1]*

Intimately intertwined with economic growth and equal rights is the topic of reproductive rights, both in the United States and around the world.

In the United States, there was a significant turning point in the case of reproductive rights, courtesy of the 1973 Supreme Court Decision of *Roe v. Wade*. The landmark decision challenged the constitutionality of laws that criminalized or restricted access to abortions, because a young woman nicknamed Jane Roe found herself pregnant in Texas in 1969, but she did not want to be. The decision to end a pregnancy is not an easy one, and the *Roe* case challenged the idea that the government can or should determine what decisions a woman can make about her body and whether she is ready or capable of carrying a pregnancy. Prior to the 1973 decision, women were not guaranteed safe and sanitary access to abortions, and many women suffered side effects from the process, including death.

While the United States has laws that protect safe and sanitary access to abortions, many countries around the world do not. Latin American countries have some of the strictest anti-abortion laws, and in some countries there are no exceptions, not even for cases of rape, incest, or abnormalities in the fetus. In South Korea, not only is abortion illegal courtesy of a law passed in 1953, but doctors who perform abortions can be charged with up to two years in prison for performing the act. Opinions are changing, and the laws are being reviewed, as they were in Ireland. In 2018, a historic referendum passed with a 66.4 percent majority in favor of repealing the Eighth Amendment, which restricted abortions in all cases in that country. Hundreds of thousands of voters registered specifically to participate in the election, and many ex-pats traveled from other nearby countries to participate in the vote.

Part of the battle for reproductive rights comes in the battle of public opinion, as there have been significant attacks made by certain groups, notably in the United States the conservative party, including President Donald Trump and Vice President Mike Pence. Trump, who re-instituted the Reagan-era anti-abortion international policy known as the Global Gag Rule not long after becoming president, has made efforts to minimize access to reproductive education and care, specifically by appointing anti-choice members to his cabinet and the judicial circuit. Additionally, the Trump administration has defunded federal educational efforts that include fact-based reproductive education in favor of abstinence-only sexual education, which has been proven to not work.

Abstinence-only education has not done enough to lower the rate of teen pregnancies in the United States—a rate which has fallen since 1990 with the efforts of fact-based education. The United States has one of the highest rates of teen pregnancy in the developed world, and not only that, but among industrialized nations, the United States also has one of the highest rates of maternal mortality, with hundreds of women dying shortly after giving birth—a rate that does not differentiate from wealth, race, or location and level of care.

Religion is also closely tied to reproductive care and also pediatric care. In Idaho, a key addition to a law passed by President Richard Nixon in 1974 to care for children who have suffered abuse has made it difficult to prosecute people like the Followers of Christ, who believe so staunchly in faith healing that they turn away all forms of modern medical care and have led to the deaths of hundreds of children who would have otherwise been able to live healthy, full lives.

Around the world, the question of a woman's right to choose, how a woman accesses reproductive care, and the importance of maintaining funding for reproductive health and education in developing countries remains a highly debated topic. While there are questions about what role religion plays in a woman's decision to choose what is right for her body and what role legal bodies have in determining abortion rights, the facts are that all women deserve not just access to reproductive care and education but to do so in a safe and sanitary environment.

In *Global Viewpoints: Reproductive Rights*, authoritative voices in the field will educate readers about all sides of the arguments and efforts being made in both the United States and abroad to protect growing populations and advance economic growth in the developing world.

Notes

1. Bjorn Anderson, "Why Reproductive Rights Are the First Step to a Freer, Fairer World," World Economic Forum, October 18, 2017.

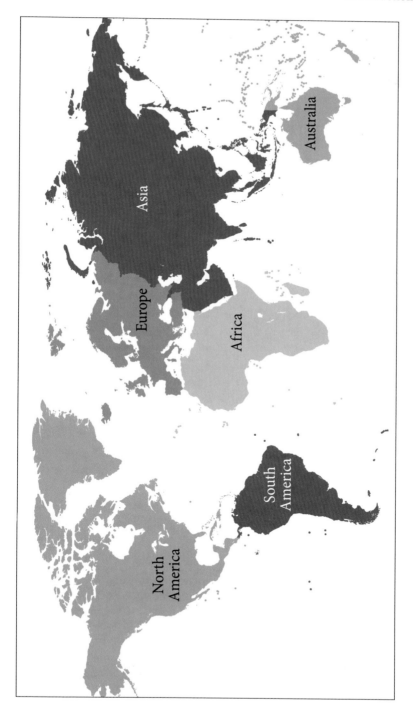

CHAPTER 1

Reproductive Rights Around the World

In the United States *Roe v. Wade* Changed Everything

Savanna Fox

In the following viewpoint, Savanna Fox details the origins behind the 1973 Supreme Court Case, Roe v. Wade. *In 1969 a woman using the pseudonym Jane Roe did not want to be pregnant but could not get an abortion where she lived, in Texas, because it was illegal in that state to do so. In the years prior to* Roe v. Wade, *hundreds of women died every year from illegal abortions gone wrong. In the years since the landmark* Roe v. Wade *decision, many states have attempted to circumvent these abortion protection mandates, and advocacy groups are attempting to combat these restrictive laws. Fox is finance and development manager at Jane's Due Process, an organization that ensures legal representation for pregnant minors in Texas.*

As you read, consider the following questions:

1. Why is there such a significant discrepancy between the number of illegal abortions women had in the years prior to *Roe v. Wade*?
2. Why do states circumvent abortion protections?
3. Why are abortions so difficult to come by for minors, people of color, people who live in rural areas, and low-income people?

"Roe v. Wade: Then, Now, and What If?" by Savanna Fox, Jane's Due Process, July 28, 2017. Reprinted by Permission.

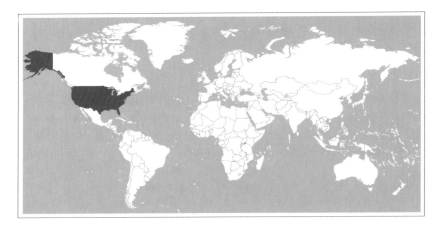

I n late 1969 a young woman in Texas was pregnant, and didn't want to be. She wanted to get an abortion, but at this time, abortion was illegal in Texas. She talked to some attorneys, and they filed a case challenging the laws that made abortion illegal. This woman was known in the court records as Jane Roe, and her case made it all the way to the Supreme Court.

In 1973 the United States Supreme Court made a decision on Jane Roe's case that has affected the lives of many people in the U.S. They decided that pregnant people have the right to legally seek abortion. The case was celebrated by many women who thought it would mean a future of safe, legal abortion for themselves and future generations. However, the decision has also allowed some states to implement restrictive abortion laws which prevent the same women from successfully getting a legal abortion today. These restrictions, which ultimately delay and dissuade people seeking a timely and safe abortion, are reminiscent of the years before *Roe v. Wade* was decided.

In the years just before *Roe v. Wade*, around 200,000 to 1.2 million women had illegal abortions each year. Illegal abortions could be highly dangerous since they were not regulated and people providing abortions didn't have to prove their medical qualifications. In addition many illegal abortions were self-induced. During this same time, roughly 200 women died per year due to illegal abortions. It is hard to get accurate numbers, because things that are illegal are often underreported. To give these numbers some context, in 2012, the CDC reported only 4 deaths associated with legal abortion for the entire year.

Court decisions are complicated, so let's break *Roe v. Wade* down. The Supreme Court determined that abortion access was protected by four amendments in the U.S. constitution. The Court decided that states are not able to ban or restrict abortions in the first trimester, and that doing so violates the first, fourth, ninth and fourteenth amendments in the U.S. constitution. The 1973 decision thus held that the right to choose to keep, or terminate, a pregnancy during the first trimester was as fundamental a right as an individuals' freedom of religion and freedom of speech, and as such it was protected from government restrictions under "strict scrutiny" requirements.

During the decision, the Supreme Court limited a state's ability to impose abortion restrictions during the first trimester. The court also acknowledged individual states' ability to protect the potential life of fetuses, but required states to justify abortion restrictions by proving it has a "compelling interest".

Despite *Roe v Wade*, officials in many states have successfully prevented abortion by passing restrictive legislation in the years since. Why is it that individual states are able to make access to safe and legal abortion so difficult to come by?

As part of their decision, the Supreme Court said that if states had a "compelling interest" in preventing abortions in the second trimester, they could pass laws restricting them. States have taken this and run with it to make abortion more difficult to obtain, and the Supreme Court has reaffirmed and expanded states' rights to do so.

In 1979, the Supreme Court held that states were able to restrict a minor's ability to access safe and legal abortion by requiring minors to get parental consent or to notify a parent. Currently, 37 states, including Texas, require minors to obtain parental consent or notify a parent before getting an abortion. In 1977, Congress

---

How Have States Circumvented Abortion Protections?

- 38 states, including Texas, require that an abortion must be performed by a licensed physician.
- 19 states require that some abortions must be performed in a hospital.
- 19 states require a second physician to participate in some abortions.
- 43 states, including Texas, prohibit abortion except in cases of life or health endangerment after a certain number of weeks (in Texas, it's 20 weeks).
- 19 states ban "partial-birth" abortion.
- 33 states, including Texas, ban public funding of abortion except in cases of life endangerment, rape or incest.
- 11 states have limited private insurance coverage of abortions.
- 45 states, including Texas, allow physicians to refuse to participate in abortions.
- 16 states, including Texas, mandate counseling information on specific topics.
- 27 states, including Texas require a waiting period after counseling.
- 37 states, including Texas, require parental involvement for minors.

DATA from the Guttmacher Institute

---

further gutted the protections offered by *Roe v. Wade* by passing the Hyde Amendment, a bill which prohibits federal Medicaid dollars from covering abortions, and in 1980, the Supreme Court declared the legislation in the Hyde Amendment constitutional. Individual states are still allowed to cover abortions with their own state dollars, but many states, including Texas, choose not to. And in 1992, during the legal battle between *Planned Parenthood of Pennsylvania v. Casey*, the Supreme Court decided that the right to abortion was no longer protected under "strict scrutiny" and instead was protected under the lesser legal requirement of "undue burden". During this same time, the Supreme Court dismantled other key abortion protections, including protections of women seeking abortion during the first trimester. This allowed states to implement required ultrasound provisions, state-mandated counseling and other restrictive elements.

In 1973 abortion access during the first trimester was a fundamental right and protected as such under the strict scrutiny requirement, meaning that states would have had to show significant and good reason for placing abortion restriction barriers on women. Now, under "undue burden", states can, and have, imposed more restrictive regulations and laws to prevent abortion. These measures are constitutional, so long as they do not pose a significant burden on women seeking abortion. Whether or not requirements like waiting periods and counseling that contradicts medical evidence are undue burdens is still up to debate—no case challenging these requirements has reached the Supreme Court yet.

How do courts decide what is significant? This is exactly the problem with undue burden: it is largely subjective and ill-defined.

Despite all of these state restrictions, abortion is still legal, though it may be hard to come by, particularly for minors, people of color, people who live in rural areas, and low-income people.

Our current presidential administration has said that they want to overturn *Roe v. Wade*. It is difficult to know exactly what would happen if *Roe v. Wade* were completely overturned. Individual states would have the discretion to implement abortion restrictions as they see fit. Some states would continue to support legal abortion, while others would not. Given Texas' track record it is safe to assume the state would implement stricter abortion laws, or make abortion illegal altogether. If *Roe v. Wade* were overturned, and states did indeed impose stricter medical regulations, making it harder for women to access safe and legal abortion, then we might return to pre-*Roe v. Wade* abortion related deaths and self-induced abortions.

The good news? Advocacy groups and abortion providers are constantly fighting against restrictive abortion laws. These people help ensure that we do not go back to pre-*Roe v. Wade* abortion related deaths. Just last summer, the Supreme Court reaffirmed the right to an abortion when it struck down key aspects of Texas

House Bill 2 (HB2). The law would have required all abortions to be performed in ambulatory surgical centers (ASCs). Such standards for abortion clinics are unnecessary, as abortion is an out-patient, low-risk procedure. Under HB2, a patient seeking a medication abortion would have had to go to a hospital-like facility with stretchers and defibrillators just to take a pill. The Supreme Court also determined that the requirements mandating physicians to have hospital admitting privileges posed an undue burden on people seeking an abortion. This was a major win, which better defined "undue burden" and put the pressure on states to have clear evidence of their compelling interest before passing abortion restrictions. Just last week, Planned Parenthood, the Center for Reproductive Rights, and Whole Women's Health filed a lawsuit against Texas regarding Senate Bill 8 (SB8), which would make dilation and evacuation, the most common second trimester abortion procedure, illegal, except in the case of an already deceased fetus. Based on the Whole Woman's Health Supreme Court decision last summer, we are optimistic about the current lawsuit challenging SB8.

It often feels like legislation regarding abortion and contraceptive coverage happen in an arena that the average citizen cannot participate in, and sometimes that is true, especially if you aren't yet of age to vote. However, it's important to remember that laws have to be voted on by your representatives. Even if you can't yet vote, you can still demonstrate your support for reproductive rights by calling or writing to your representative, attending a lobby day at the Capitol during the legislative session, and talking to your friends about why supporting abortion access is important to you.

In the United States Before *Roe v. Wade* Abortions Were Life-Threatening

Marie Solis and Jo Baxter

In the following viewpoint, Marie Solis tells the story of Jo Baxter, who found herself pregnant in 1965, at age twenty. At the time, abortion was illegal in Nebraska—as it was in most of the United States. That did not stop her from making the decision to end a pregnancy she knew she could not support at such a young age. Considering what happened to a close family member whose life was impacted by an unintended pregnancy that forced her to leave school and ultimately changed her life, Baxter and her boyfriend made the decision to seek out a chiropractor from Kansas who helped her end the pregnancy. Solis writes about politics and women's issues at Newsweek.

As you read, consider the following questions:

1. According to the viewpoint, why did Baxter choose to end her pregnancy?
2. Why was it important for women like Baxter to have the ability to make the decision she made?
3. How does the lack of a right to choose what is right for her body impact a woman's life and career?

Jo Baxter, as told to Marie Solis, "What It Was Like Getting an Abortion Before Roe v. Wade" Broadly, July 5, 2018, *Vice* Media. Reprinted by Permission.

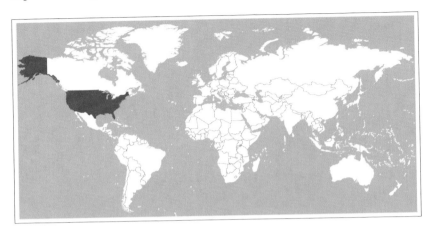

I knew I was pregnant the minute I missed my period. I don't even know if we had at-home pregnancy tests at the time—if we did, I don't remember using one. I just knew I was pregnant. It was 1965, and I was about 20 years old, in my junior year at the University of Nebraska studying journalism. I had no hesitation about getting an abortion.

I grew up in a very conservative, religious family, and in those days the only option for someone who got pregnant—at least as far as my parents were concerned—was to get married. Well, my boyfriend and I weren't ready to get married, and we certainly weren't ready to be parents. And I didn't want to go through what I had seen my relatives go through—particularly one close relative, who was extremely bright and got pregnant her first semester of college. Her parents forced her to get married and she dropped out of school to raise her children. I'm convinced that if she had finished college and had a family later on, gotten an education and started her career, she would've had an entirely different life. I didn't want to be in that boat, and I didn't want my parents to feel that their daughter had let them down by getting pregnant out of wedlock, which was a serious sin in their eyes.

But the main thing that drove me to get the abortion was very personal—I simply did not want to have a child at that point. I knew some day I wanted to, but not then.

My boyfriend happened to know someone. He had a colleague at work who had once stopped on the side of the road to help a man who was stranded change a flat tire. When he was finished, the man handed him a business card and said, "If you ever get a girl in trouble, here's my card." He was a chiropractor in Kansas. I called him and said, "I need some help"—I don't even think I said "I need an abortion." It was so illegal I was afraid to be too specific, but I think he could tell immediately why I was calling. He performed abortions on the weekends, when he wasn't seeing patients, and he told me to come in on a Saturday.

At the time I was living in a sorority house, and we had a curfew. I had to sneak out of the house in the middle of the night to meet my boyfriend and his friend, who had a car and whom we'd convinced to drive us the six or seven hours it would take to get there.

I had no idea what was going to happen to me. We didn't have the internet to look up what an abortion was, or what it entailed. I didn't know anyone who had gotten an abortion, and I didn't tell anyone I was getting one, except for the people who came with me. But I was a very determined woman, and I was going to go through with it even though I had no clue what to expect.

When we got to the chiropractor's office, he took me up to a room where he had an exam table with stirrups and a speculum. I don't remember now much of what was said between the two of us, but I got the sense that he was experienced at it. I didn't know it at the time, but I later realized what I ended up having was a D&C, or dilation and curettage, abortion. I wasn't given any anesthesia or painkillers. The chiropractor told me that I would pass the fetus in about 24 hours, and that if I started bleeding I should get myself to a hospital right away.

I don't recall the procedure itself being painful, but I do remember being in a tremendous amount of pain on the car ride home from the cramps caused by the D&C. By the time I got back to the sorority house, though, the worst of the cramping had passed and I was able to walk in like nothing happened. That night or

One Step Backward?

The Country Report on Human Rights Practices (CRHRP), compiled and submitted to Congress every year by the State Department, provides a detailed account of the status of human rights policies around the world. But the 2018 report—the first to be released under the Trump Administration—was missing something. This year, the CRHRP didn't include coverage of reproductive health and rights.

In 2012, then-Secretary of State Hillary Clinton added to the CRHRP a designated section on reproductive rights, requiring the department to evaluate abortion access, contraception and maternal and child health overseas and include their data in the final report. Under Clinton's leadership and in the years that followed, the CRHRP provided a well-rounded overview of women's reproductive rights across the globe—including information on whether the general population is able to freely practice their reproductive rights, existing policies affecting or pertaining to reproductive rights in that country and any barriers, threats, concerns or failures to uphold reproductive rights by state governments.

Now, for the first time in six years, the report doesn't include any detailed information on the status of global reproductive rights—except for one section titled "coercion in population control," which harkens back to earlier claims by the administration that the United Nations Population Fund (UNFPA), which lost $32.5 million in funding from the U.S. under Trump's leadership, participates in coercive abortion policies and forced sterilizations in tandem with the Chinese government. That wasn't true then, and evidently is not true now.

The Trump administration's disregard for women's human rights abroad, and in particular their access to reproductive and sexual heath care, is by now par for the course. "Omitting [this] issue," Amnesty International said in a statement about the CRHRP, "signals the Trump administration's latest retreat from global leadership on human rights." It certainly wasn't Trump's first—and women in the U.S. and abroad have no reason to believe it will be his last.

This administration can do their best to erase women's rights, but women won't go back. And as Clinton herself famously declared: reproductive rights are (still) human rights, whether federal officials want to admit as much or not.

"Reproductive Rights are Still Human Rights—Even if the Trump Administration Won't Say So," by Tiernan Hebron, Ms. Magazine, May 2, 2018.

some time the next day I passed the fetus, just like he said. And I felt this amazing relief.

I have not ever, ever regretted it for one second.

I ended up marrying my boyfriend soon after, and we had our first son together when I was 25. We were both older, we could afford it—we both had jobs working at newspapers—and I knew I would have the assistance of my husband raising him. I later went into public relations and spent the majority of my career as a chief marketing officer in Florida. We had another son, and now each of them have two daughters. Next week, my husband and I will celebrate our 52nd wedding anniversary.

I'm quite certain I wouldn't have been able to finish school or have the career I did if I hadn't had the abortion, and that would've been an utterly different life. I loved working. I loved having a professional career. I don't see any other path that would've led me to where I was ultimately able to go.

I was so happy when the *Roe v. Wade* decision came down years after my abortion. I can't tell you how happy I felt over thinking about how women wouldn't have to go through what I went through. I thought about how if I ever had a daughter, she wouldn't have to make this kind of a decision without knowing she had some way to receive care that was safe and legal. I didn't have any daughters, but I did have four granddaughters, and now I'm so concerned that if *Roe* is overturned, they'll end up in the same circumstance I was at some point in their lives.

I got lucky: My abortion wasn't necessarily safe, and it definitely wasn't legal, but I came out of it OK. I just hope that other women who've had abortions will be willing to talk about their experience. People need to understand that having an abortion isn't an uncommon thing, and just how critically important access to abortion is.

No one other than a woman should be able to decide what happens to her own body. Someone in my shoes might have made a completely different decision, and that would've been the right thing for them. But it wasn't for me. Every woman has to decide for herself what's best.

In Ireland Citizens Vote "Yes" to Legalize Abortion in Landslide Referendum

James Hitchings-Hales

In the following viewpoint, James Hitchings-Hales details the 2018 referendum that Ireland voted for to legalize abortion in the country. The highly publicized referendum to repeal language in Ireland's Eighth Amendment passed with 66.4 percent of voters in favor of the legalization. Prior to the vote, all abortions in Ireland were illegal and had been since 1861. This ban on abortions included those in cases of rape, incest, or fetal abnormality. The referendum is the first step toward legalizing unrestricted abortions on pregnancies up to twelve weeks. Hitchings-Hales is a digital/communications assistant at Global Citizen.

As you read, consider the following questions:

1. Why was turnout so high in the vote for this referendum?
2. Compared to the sixty-five thousand new voters who registered for Ireland's vote on same-sex marriage, how many more new voters registered for this referendum?
3. What is the reasoning behind the opposition to the referendum? Is it valid? Why or why not?

"Ireland Votes 'Yes' to Legalise Abortion in Landslide Referendum," by James Hitchings-Hales, Global Poverty Project, Inc., May 26, 2018.

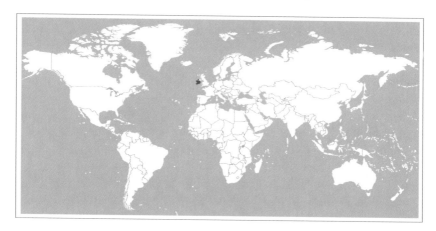

The Republic of Ireland has voted decisively to repeal a key constitutional clause that restricts abortion rights in a historic referendum that has grasped the attention of the world.

The landslide victory means Ireland will now take steps to legalise abortion during the first 12 weeks of pregnancy.

With results in from all 40 constituencies, the final result stands at 66.4% "yes" and 33.6% "no."

It's currently illegal to terminate pregnancy in Ireland including in cases of rape, incest, or abnormality in the foetus, and it's punishable by up to 14 years in prison for both the recipient and the medical professional who carries it out.

As a result, hundreds of thousands of women in recent decades have travelled abroad to secure a termination. Approximately 3,500 women do so every year, often to the UK, while 2,000 self-medicate with illegal abortion pills annually, according to the Guardian.

Abortion has been permissible if a woman's life is in danger since 2014, following public outcry at the death of 31-year-old Savita Halappanavar, who lost her life after a lengthy miscarriage. Now, legislation will plan to permit abortions on pregnancies up to 24 weeks if there's a threat to the mother's life.

Leo Varadkar, Ireland's Taoiseach—a title used to describe the Irish head of government—had earlier said that the referendum was a "once in a generation decision." If the result had been different, another vote would have been unlikely for at least 35 years, he said.

In response to an Irish Times exit poll that last night predicted a 68%–32% win for the "yes" campaign, Varadkar described the result as "democracy in action."

But it's a campaign that has been fiercely fought by both sides.

"There are people who are deeply broken-hearted at this outcome," said John McGuirk, communications director at Save the 8th, a leading anti-abortion campaign. An official statement earlier conceded defeat, describing the loss as a "tragedy of historic proportions."

What Was Ireland Voting For?

The focus of the debate was a specific article in the Irish constitution, known as the eighth amendment, that grants "equal right to life" between a pregnant mother and her unborn foetus.

Abortion has been illegal in Ireland since 1861. But a 1983 referendum sought to enshrine the ban in the constitution, and comfortably won. There were further referendums in 1992 and 2002 to establish, amongst other things, whether suicidal thoughts could be grounds for abortion, and on both occasions the suggestion was defeated. From 2014 a new law permitted abortion to protect loss of life, including from suicide.

The ballot paper for this referendum did not actually mention abortion, instead asking: "Do you approve of the proposal to amend the Constitution contained in the undermentioned Bill?"

The winning pro-choice "yes" vote fought for a repeal of the article in order to pass legislation to legalise unrestricted abortions on pregnancies up to 12 weeks. The losing pro-life "no" campaign fought to retain it.

With the final result confirmed, the constitution is now set to change.

How Many People Voted?

Over 3.2 million people were registered to vote, according to the Department of Housing and Local Government. It includes over 100,000 new voters who joined the register in the run-up to the referendum, more than the 65,000 who joined for the same-sex marriage vote.

It's reported that turnout was up to 70% in some areas, with figures from a number of polling stations showing a stronger turnout than the 2015 marriage equality referendum—which had a turnout of 61%.

Many travelled thousands of miles to return to Ireland and cast their ballot. Viral stories on social media revealed that some had flown from Argentina, Los Angeles, Australia, and more to have their say on the result.

How Has the Country Reacted?

The online reaction has reflected the result. The "yes" camp were jubilant with the result, with celebrations spilling out into the streets across the country.

"This is a resounding roar from the Irish people for repealing the 8th amendment," said Orla O'Connor, co-director for leading repeal campaign Together for Yes.

However, "no" campaigners expressed regret at the decision, and reiterated their commitment to oppose any new legislation and the formation of abortion clinics in the country.

"Every time an unborn child has his or her life ended in Ireland, we will oppose that, and make our voices known," read an official statement from Save the 8th. "Abortion was wrong yesterday. It remains wrong today. The constitution has changed, but the facts have not."

What Are the Next Steps?

First, the eighth amendment will be replaced with the words: "Provision may be made by law for the regulation of termination of pregnancy."

This amends the constitution, but not the original law passed in 1861. Draft legislation will then be submitted to parliament to replace it. You can view the policy paper here.

Despite certain opposition, the legislation is expected to pass, and abortion for pregnancies up to 12 weeks will become legal in Ireland. Experts anticipate it could become legal before the end of the year.

The Guardian reports that the result will have far reaching consequences across the world, and could inspire activists fighting for abortion rights internationally. It's currently illegal in Northern Ireland in all but the most extreme circumstances, but it's expected that there will now be mounting pressure for similar change.

In Latin America Women Are Punished for Their Abortions

Verónica Osorio Calderón and Kristof Decoster

In the following viewpoint, Verónica Osorio Calderón and Kristof Decoster detail the incredibly restrictive anti-abortion laws in Latin American countries, which have led to millions of abortions being performed in unsafe and highly unsanitary conditions. While the risks for abortions are high, the costs are equally as high if women are caught, as there are strict punishments for abortions, including jail sentences as high as forty years in El Salvador and fifty years in Mexico. Part of the reason why there are such strict punishments is that women in these countries are seen as mothers and that society forces women to continue pregnancies no matter the cost or a woman's right to decide otherwise.

As you read, consider the following questions:

1. Per the viewpoint, how many abortions occurred in Latin American countries every year between 2010 and 2014?
2. Despite the fact that the UN Human Rights Commission has declared safe abortion a human right, why are 95 percent of abortions in Latin America performed in unsanitary conditions?
3. What are the main causes of death from unsafe abortions? Are they preventable? Why or why not?

"The right to health and safe abortion in Latin America: still a long way to go", by Verónica Osorio Calderón and Kristof Decoster, *International Health Policies*, September 29, 2017. Reprinted by permission.

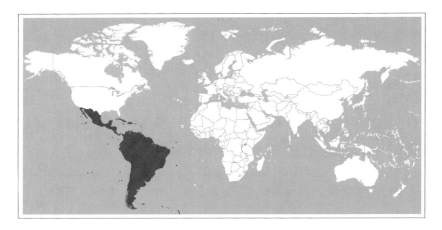

I n Latin America, an estimated 6.5 million abortions occurred every year between 2010 and 2014, with 95% of them performed clandestinely in unsafe and unsanitary conditions, representing 10% of maternal mortality in the region. As of today, only four countries in Latin America allow assisted abortion in all circumstances; in six countries it is not permitted for any reason, while the rest of the countries accept assisted abortion under certain circumstances. Despite the risks, Latin American women continue to undergo unsafe abortions and the region remains with the strictest and most restrictive laws and norms in the world on this issue. The right to safe abortion to avoid deaths, as well as sexual education and family planning to avoid abortions have become very polarized debates in Latin America, with endless discussion in social and political spheres.

Although the UN Human Rights Commission declared safe abortion a human right, in most Latin American countries it remains a decision of the State. Legalization does not lead to an increase in abortions, but neither does it lead to a decrease. The only way to reduce abortion is through family planning, and thus sexual education is more than necessary, but this does not prevent women from looking for abortion if needed. This is why it is vital to legalize abortion and recognize it as a women's human right. Various UN special rapporteurs have called for decriminalization of and access to safe abortion services. In Latin America, in the absence of this, hundreds of women still die every year under painful and dishonourable situations due to clandestine abortions, even if in recent years the region has seen fewer deaths and severe complications from unsafe abortions as it is increasingly common for (at least some) Latin American women to obtain and self-administer medicines like misoprostol outside of formal health systems.

Death and disabilities in women due to abortion are preventable. The main causes of death because of unsafe abortion are related to haemorrhage, infection, and poisoning; morbidity results from complications related to haemorrhage, sepsis, peritonitis, and trauma to the cervix, vagina, uterus, and abdominal organs. In addition, symptoms of mental health problems related to the unsafe abortion often also occur such as anxiety, depression, impulse-control problems, ... and other mental disorders. If abortion were legalized, women would have timely access to healthcare and an adequate and safe abortion, if needed. They could also receive counselling from professional staff.

Despite the costs and impact on women's health, laws and norms in the region are extremely strict for women who have an abortion. Latin American countries are failing to support women facing these difficulties but they punish them without considering their reasons to abort. For example, in El Salvador, jail sentences are as high as 40 years when a woman aborts and 50 years in Mexico, even if these abortions were not voluntary; in Paraguay, an 11-year old sexually abused child delivered a baby after she was denied abortion in 2015; in Brazil, 33 women were arrested, accused of abortion, during 2014. Seven of them were denounced by healthcare staff who provided them services; in Argentina, abortion is the main cause of maternal death. There are many similar cases in other countries in the region.

Strong cultural beliefs and traditions still influence health policy making, especially in sensitive areas such as abortion. The role of women as mothers in the society forces women to continue pregnancies despite the many reasons they could have to stop their pregnancy. From the point of view of gender equality, women and men should be given the same opportunities and chances "to access and control social, economic and political resources, including protection under the law (such as health services, education and voting rights)". However, when men cause an abortion by abandoning or denying a pregnant woman there is no equal punishment (nor the same stigmatization); needless to say, men also do not get pregnant after sexual assault. Society expects women to take responsibility and punishes her if she does not.

This Latin American idiosyncrasy was also on full display during the Zika epidemic. Pregnant women infected with the Zika virus had an increased risk of microcephaly in newborns, hence pregnant women were the target population. Governments recommended women to avoid pregnancy during the next two years, and after acknowledging the link between the virus and sexual transmission, they also provided information on the use of contraception. However, this information did not include comprehensive sexual education that could have led to conscious family planning as it was focused on the epidemic only. It was not considered that women are typically in charge of the caring tasks and that microcephaly requires full time care and financing, affecting mostly women who are mothers of the affected children. No country in the region legalized abortion during that time.

So it's a fact: far too many women still die and have disabilities due to unsafe abortions and this harm can only be prevented by providing timely health services and family planning. So, instead of penalizing it, governments should guarantee access to safe abortion to all women without discrimination, and provide comprehensive sexual education to decrease the number of abortions. There has been little progress so far on this matter in the region. Still, Uruguay made safe abortion accessible in 2012, and Chile just passed a bill that allows women to abort for medical reasons or when pregnancy is a consequence of rape. On the downside, we are yet to see the full extent of the negative impact of the reinstatement of the Global

Gag Rule in Latin American countries. Trump's policy will affect Central America more than South America, it is predicted.

In short, there is still a long way to go. Latin America society and governments need to understand that besides a public health problem, safe abortion is a human right. Hence, the first step to take is to legalize abortion in order to provide it as a health service and avoid deaths. As the 29th Pan-American Sanitary Conference is wrapping up, we are crossing fingers that someone will have dared to bring this issue up in the discussions. In the meantime, what we can do is to stand up for ourselves and join one of the actions and events happening globally to demand the right to safe abortion.

In South Korea a Half-Century-Year-Old Abortion Ban Needs Another Look

Kelly Kasulis

In the following viewpoint, Kelly Kasulis details the push for South Korea's Constitutional Court to review the ban on abortion that the nation passed in 1953. The impetus on the review started from a doctor who was prosecuted for performing nearly seventy abortions over the course of two years because he believes that the law endangers women's health. In South Korea, an estimated one in five women have had an abortion, and 45 percent of youth in South Korea are unaware that such a ban exists. In rural areas, abortions come at an extremely high cost, up to 5 million won or $4,620.

As you read, consider the following questions:

1. Other than religion, what are the reasons why some people in South Korea are against abortion?
2. How has the #MeToo movement impacted the women's equality movements in South Korea?
3. Per the viewpoint, what are the reasons why South Korea's abortion law is flawed?

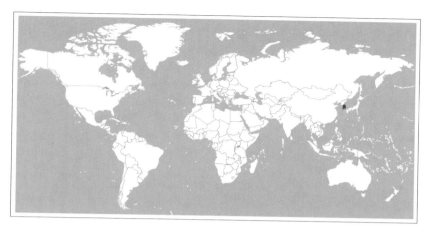

S outh Korea's Constitutional Court is reviewing the nation's 1953 abortion ban, which makes abortion punishable by up to a year in prison or a fine up to 2 million won (about $1,850). And that's for the women. There are even harsher punishments for doctors—up to two years in prison—which is actually why it's under review in the first place. After being prosecuted for conducting nearly 70 abortions over the course of two years, a South Korean doctor decided to challenge the law, saying it endangers women's health.

"This isn't just whether or not you're going to jail. It's about how hard it is for women to get a safe abortion and protect their health," said Ryu Min-hee, core counsel on the case and an attorney at Korean Lawyers for Public Interest and Human Rights. "We hope that the constitutional court of Korea will make the right decision on this, because it's long overdue."

These days, any topic related to women's rights is part of a greater moment in South Korea, a historically patriarchal society with a burgeoning feminist movement. More than 12,000 women marched in Seoul on May 19 to protest police bias against women who report sexual crimes; seas of demonstrators held up #MeToo signs on International Women's Day in March. Both protests were met with severe criticism online and off, sparking concern about demonstrator safety—one man was even arrested outside of the May police bias rally for threatening to attack women with hydrochloric acid.

More than 235,000 people signed a Blue House petition last year calling for an end to the abortion ban, but public opinion overall appears to be divided. According to an October 2016 survey of 1,018 people, about 53 percent of South Koreans believe abortion is morally "a kind of murder." About 73 percent of respondents knew of the abortion ban. The stark anti-abortion sentiment is in a steep decline—in 1994, 78 percent of people surveyed called it a type of murder. But none of this means the ban will be overturned.

Aside from the usual conservative Christian bloc, some are against abortion because they believe it exacerbates South Korea's dangerously low birth rate.

"The idea that it's going to improve birth rate by forcing women to have babies they don't want is ludicrous. Research shows that doesn't work at all. When you ban an abortion, people still have abortions—just unsafe ones," said Heather Barr, senior researcher on women's rights for Human Rights Watch. "If I were the South Korean government and I was worried about the aging population, I would be thinking aggressively about how to make people who want children feel like they can afford it."

"I think it's actually about being against women's sexuality and lives—the freedom to choose," Ryu said. "During our public hearing for the case, the government—they sent me this legal briefing that says, 'If you have sexual intercourse, you should know there will be some kind of consequence like abortion, and you should be responsible for the consequences.' We were surprised to hear that argument."

A Poorly Written Law

As it's written, South Korea's current abortion law is flawed, ineffective and arbitrarily enforced—which is a problem on both sides of the debate. Illegal abortions are already happening at high rates, for example—an estimated 1 in 5 pregnant women have had one, according to the Korean Women's Development Institute.

The practice is widespread partly because lawmakers historically turned a blind eye to it. In the 1960s and 1970s, the national government ran numerous "family planning" campaigns in hopes that reducing the population would address post-war poverty. Illegal abortions were fairly commonplace—between 1960 and 2016, the fertility rate dropped from 6.1 children per woman to 1.12. And by 1994, some 45 percent of South Koreans surveyed by Gallup Korea incorrectly thought that the ban didn't exist.

"In the 1960s and 1970s, people were actually encouraged to limit their reproductive capacity in various ways," Ryu said. "They really arbitrarily enforced this criminal provision before, when they felt like we had too much of a population. Now, the government feels we have too little of a population."

Another issue with the abortion ban: Abortions are only permitted in the case of married women. Women who are eligible for an abortion under one of a limited number exceptions still need their husband's permission.

The 1953 law allows abortion in the case of rape, incest, the possibility of passing on certain hereditary diseases and the possibility that pregnancy can cause serious health conditions for the pregnant female. These circumstances are incredibly rare —2005 data showed that the exceptions only applied to about 4 percent of the 340,000 abortions performed.

That "doesn't really make any sense," Ryu said. Because the law asks for a husband's permission specifically, it's unclear whether unmarried women can get approval for abortions.

That makes the law relatively easy for spiteful husbands to abuse. "This clause is actually sometimes misused by the husband to blackmail women after their abortion. We have several cases like that," Ryu said.

Women Can't Win

When it comes to reproductive rights and family planning, South Korean women are in a particularly difficult spot. Being a single mother is highly stigmatized, as is adoption of those children

---

China's New Rules

New rules restricting abortions in a Chinese province have prompted concern from citizens and activists over state control of women's bodies.

Jiangxi province issued guidelines last week stipulating that women more than 14 weeks pregnant must have signed approval from three medical professionals confirming an abortion is medically necessary before any procedure. The measures are meant to help prevent sex-selective abortions, which are illegal in China.

"Your womb is being monitored," said one comment on the Weibo microblogging website. "What is the purpose and basis of this policy? The reproductive rights of women in this country seem to be a joke," said another. One user wrote simply, "The Handmaid's Tale," referring to the TV series set in a dystopian future where women's reproductive functions are tightly controlled by the state.

Jiangxi's guidelines come as Chinese officials look for ways to deal with the country's ageing population and low fertility rates, the result of decades of restricting family size, known as the one-child policy.

Loosened restrictions over recent years to allow all parents to have two children has so far failed to resolve China's demographic problems, which threatens economic growth.

Some worry China's family planning apparatus will turn its heavy-handed approach to restricting women's choices.

---

within the country (many South Korean adoptees end up abroad). Pregnant women who don't want either outcome may have no choice but to get an underground abortion, which puts them at serious health risk. On the abortion black market, records are hardly ever kept and doctors are immune to legal consequences from a botched procedure.

"The complications of a bad abortion include death. Hemorrhaging—a lot of things can happen," Barr said. "There's no safe way to have an illegal abortion. It's a serious medical procedure that needs to be performed by competent, trained professionals."

Even if abortions are legalized, it will take some time for South Korea's medical community to catch up.

"People are worried that the government will go from lifting restrictions, to encouraging reproduction, to imposing restrictions on abortion and restricting people's own decisions," said Lu Pin, founder of Feminist Voices, a blog on gender issues.

Lu added that many Chinese women, who had chosen not to have a second child despite the new policies, were fearful that strict social policies will be introduced. "There are plenty of signs that show their worries are not unfounded," she said.

China's family planning policies have long encouraged the use of abortions, along with contraceptives and sterilisation, as a way to restrict population growth. Since 1971, when the country first introduced limits, doctors have performed 336m abortions, according to government data released in 2013.

In the past, other provinces have implemented similar rules to crack down on aborting female foetuses, a practice that has left China with a massive gender imbalance of 30 million more men than women.

In 2004, Guizhou was the first province to enact such a ban. Other Chinese provinces such as Jiangsu, Hunan, Qinghai, Anhui, Henan, and the city of Shanghai have followed suit with varying restrictions on abortions after 14 weeks.

"China: new rules to prevent sex-selective abortions raise fears," by Lily Kuo, Guardian News and Media Limited, June 22, 2018.

"Doctors cannot get any proper education at medical school because legal abortion is so narrow, and they don't get that experience during their internships or their residency," Ryu said. "When you live in a rural area and you are underage, it's hard for you to find a doctor that is willing to perform the operation."

She added that women in rural areas are likely charged more for illegal abortions. In general, fees for underground abortions can be as high as 5 million won (about $4,620), according to an expert witness in the case. In comparison, abortions in the US can range from a few hundred dollars to as much as about $3,000.

For now, advocates for legal abortion are forced to wait. There's no telling how quickly the Constitutional Court will reach a decision, nor is there a deadline for a verdict. But in a time when public opinion is rapidly shifting in favor of women's equality and women's rights, it's certainly possible that 2018 will be a year of change in South Korea.

"I honestly can't predict [an outcome]. I can only hope," Ryu said. "I see a lot of opinions supportive of abortion from the public. They understand that it's about women's autonomy and their choices about their lives."

Periodical and Internet Sources Bibliography

The following articles have been selected to supplement the diverse views presented in this chapter.

Eve Andrews, "The Trump Administration's Climate Report Left Out Reproductive Rights. Here's What It Missed." *Mother Jones*, December 2, 2018. https://www.motherjones.com/environment/2018/12/the-trump-administrations-climate-report-left-out-reproductive-rights-heres-what-it-missed/.

Associated Foreign Press, "Calls to end South Korea abortion ban reach top court," *Straits Times*, May 22, 2018. https://www.straitstimes.com/asia/east-asia/calls-to-end-south-korea-abortion-ban-reach-top-court.

BBC.com, "Irish abortion referendum: Ireland overturns abortion ban," BBC.com, May 28, 2018. https://www.bbc.com/news/world-europe-44256152.

Amanda Michelle Gomez, "Anti-abortion groups ask SCOTUS to reconsider Roe v. Wade and uphold Mike Pence's anti-choice law," Think Progress, November 30, 2018. https://thinkprogress.org/anti-abortion-groups-scotus-roe-v-wade-uphold-mike-pence-d96e260d8de2/.

John Henley, "What you need to know: the Irish abortion referendum explained," *Guardian*, May 25, 2018. https://www.theguardian.com/world/2018/may/25/irish-abortion-referendum-explained-what-you-need-to-know.

Dan Horn, "The Willke Way: How a Cincinnati couple put Roe v. Wade on the ropes," Cincinnati.com, November 24, 2018. https://www.cincinnati.com/story/news/politics/2018/11/24/roe-v-wade-how-cincinnati-couple-took-legalized-abortion/1856988002/.

Annie Kelly, "Latin America's fight to legalise abortion: the key battlegrounds," *Guardian*, August 9, 2018. https://www.theguardian.com/global-development/2018/aug/09/latin-america-fight-to-legalise-abortion-argentina-brazil-chile-venezuela-uruguay-colombia-el-salvador-peru.

Hong-Ji Kim, "South Korea: Decriminalize Abortion," Human Rights Watch, May 23,2018. https://www.hrw.org/news/2018/05/23/south-korea-decriminalize-abortion.

Ciara Nugent, "Argentina Votes Today on Legalizing Abortion. Here's What That Means for Women's Rights Across Latin America," *Time*, August 7, 2018. http://time.com/5358823/argentina-abortion-vote-latin-america/.

Alice Miranda Ollstein, "Here come the Roe v. Wade challenges," Politico, November 8, 2018. https://www.politico.com/story/2018/11/08/abortion-roe-v-wade-abortion-court-cases-supreme-court-944166.

Mokoto Rich, "Push to End South Korea Abortion Ban Gains Strength, and Signatures," *New York Times*, January 13, 2018. https://www.nytimes.com/2018/01/13/world/asia/south-korea-abortion-ban.html.

Madhury Sathish, "Where Is Abortion Legal In Latin America? Laws In The Region Are Extremely Strict," Bustle, August 9, 2018. https://www.bustle.com/p/where-is-abortion-legal-in-latin-america-laws-in-the-region-are-extremely-strict-10064072.

CHAPTER 2

Societal Impressions of Reproductive Rights

In the United States the Supreme Court's Hobby Lobby Ruling Allows Companies Exemption from Providing Contraceptives

Mary Agnes Carey

In the following viewpoint, Mary Agnes Carey details the result of the 2014 Supreme Court case filed by Hobby Lobby Stores and Conestoga Wood Specialties. Hobby Lobby stated that for-profit companies should not have to provide approved contraceptive services for its employees, as some of these contraceptives violate their owners' religious beliefs. The case passed in a 5-4 decision, and means that Hobby Lobby will not have to pay fines totaling over $500 million dollars a year for excluding some forms of birth control on its health plans. Carey is senior correspondent for Kaiser Health News.

As you read, consider the following questions:

1. According to the viewpoint, what forms of contraception were Hobby Lobby and Conestoga objecting to and why?
2. Should the 1993 Religious Freedom Restoration Act allow companies to interfere with a woman's right to choose her preferred method of contraception?
3. Why is it important that the Supreme Court's decision is so narrow?

"Hobby Lobby Ruling Cuts into Contraceptive Mandate", by Mary Agnes Carey, Henry J. Kaiser Family Foundation, June 30, 2014. Reprinted by permission.

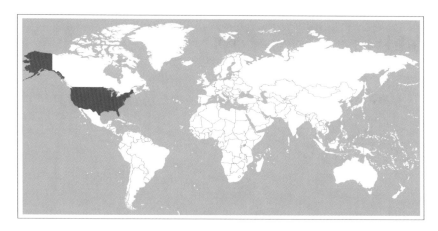

In a 5-4 decision Monday, the Supreme Court allowed a key exemption to the health law's contraception coverage requirements when it ruled that closely held for-profit businesses could assert a religious objection to the Obama administration's regulations. What does it mean? Here are some questions and answers about the case.

What Did the Court's Ruling Do?

The court's majority said that the for-profit companies that filed suit—Hobby Lobby Stores, a nationwide chain of 500 arts and crafts stores, and Conestoga Wood Specialties, a maker of custom cabinets—didn't have to offer female employees all Food and Drug Administration-approved contraceptives as part of a package of preventive services that must be covered without copays or deductibles under the law. The companies had argued that several types of contraceptives violate their owners' religious beliefs. The ruling also covers a Hobby Lobby subsidiary, the Mardel Christian bookstores.

What Does the Health Law Say About Contraception Coverage?

As part of the law's coverage of preventive health services, health insurance plans are required to cover all FDA-approved contraception methods for women without any cost-sharing, such as deductibles or copayments. Those methods include birth control pills, intrauterine devices and sterilization procedures. Employers with 50 or more workers that offer coverage that doesn't meet that standard would face fines of $100 a day per worker. These large employers that don't offer any coverage face a fine of $2,000 for most employees. The contraceptive guidelines apply to women only.

Writing for the majority, Justice Samuel Alito stated that Hobby Lobby would have faced fines of $475 million a year and Conestoga $33 million for excluding some forms of birth control from their health plans. If the employers had decided to drop coverage altogether, Hobby Lobby would have paid roughly $26 million in penalties and Conestoga $1.8 million, far less than the fine for not covering all FDA-approved methods of birth control.

The Department of Health and Human Services set the contraception requirement based on an Institute of Medicine study that recommended prescription contraception and services, including all FDA-approved methods of contraception, be included as preventive services for women. Most health plans had to cover contraceptive services for plan years beginning on or after Aug. 1, 2012, according to HHS. Grandfathered plans that hadn't changed significantly after the health law passed do not have to offer preventive health care—including contraception—without cost-sharing.

Why Did These Companies Bring Suit?

Hobby Lobby and Conestoga are family-owned, and they said that the health law's contraception requirement violated their religious views. While both employers' health plans cover some forms of birth control, the employers object to emergency contraceptives such as Plan B and Ella that can prevent a pregnancy if taken within a short window after unprotected sex. The owners contend that these contraceptive methods prevent a fertilized egg from implanting in the woman's uterus and therefore are a type of abortion. Hobby Lobby's owners also object to two types of intrauterine devices, or IUDs, for the same reason.

Supreme Court Justice Gorusch's Record Regarding Reproductive Rights

Round one in the battle against the birth control benefit was brought by arts-and-crafts giant Hobby Lobby, and other for-profit companies, which had a religious objection to providing contraception coverage in their employees' health plan. Before Hobby Lobby's case reached the Supreme Court, the Court of Appeals for the Tenth Circuit ruled in favor of Hobby Lobby. In that decision, Judge Gorsuch wrote a separate opinion to underscore that the family that owns Hobby Lobby would be complicit in sin if it allowed their employees' health insurance company to cover contraception.

Although the Supreme Court narrowly sided with Hobby Lobby, ... the court noted that the government already had a system in place for religiously affiliated non-profit organizations that allowed those employers to opt-out of paying for contraception coverage by filling out a simple form, and instead the health insurance company would pay for the contraception coverage.

Round two in the battle against the birth control benefit was brought by a nursing home called Little Sisters of the Poor Home for the Aged, and other religiously affiliated non-profit organizations. Those employers objected to the opt-out system itself, arguing that filling out the form to opt out of providing contraception violated their religious beliefs. Eight of the nine courts of appeals to consider these challenges, including the Tenth Circuit, held that filling out a form did not substantially burden the employers' religious beliefs. But Judge Gorsuch joined an opinion arguing that the Tenth Circuit should reconsider the decision in the Little Sisters of the Poor case siding, once again, with the employer.

Judge Gorsuch's disregard for the effect on women in these cases is troubling. If an employer blocks its employees' access to contraception coverage, that employer is discriminating based on sex. Women already pay more for health care than men, and the contraception coverage requirement was designed to reduce that disparity. Equally important, contraception is crucial for women's equal participation in society. Being able to decide whether and when to have children has a direct effect on women's ability to make their own paths in terms of their schooling, their careers, and their families.

"Should Your Boss's Religious Beliefs Dictate Your Health Insurance Coverage? Supreme Court Nominee Judge Gorsuch Thinks So," by Brigitte Amiri, ACLU, February 2, 2017.

The companies argued that they should be exempted from the contraceptive requirement because the 1993 Religious Freedom Restoration Act, or RFRA, says that the government may not pose a "substantial burden" on the free exercise of religion unless that burden is the narrowest possible way to further a compelling government interest. The federal government and advocates for the health law's contraception requirements argued that only individuals—not corporations—can exercise religious rights.

Does Everyone Agree That the Contraceptives That Hobby Lobby and Conestaga Object to Cause Abortions?

No. U.S. Solicitor General Donald Verrilli said during the oral arguments in the case on behalf of the Obama administration, "Federal law and State law—which do preclude funding for abortions—don't consider these particular forms of contraception to be abortion."

A brief filed by 10 medical groups led by the American College of Obstetricians and Gynecologists noted "there is a scientific distinction between a contraceptive and an abortifacient and the scientific record demonstrates that none of the FDA-approved contraceptives covered by the Mandate are abortifacients."

That's because the standard medical definition of the start of pregnancy is when a fertilized egg implants in a woman's uterus, not when sperm and egg first unite.

But while blocking implantation of a fertilized egg doesn't fit the medical definition of pregnancy, it does qualify as ending a life for many religious people.

Are There Any Religious Exceptions from the Health Law's Contraception Mandate?

Churches and other houses of worship are exempt from the requirement to provide contraceptive services at no cost to employees. However, religious-affiliated institutions, such as universities and hospitals, would have to provide coverage for all FDA-approved contraceptive methods. Those organizations objecting to such coverage can turn to a third party, such as an insurer, to cover the cost of contraception, under a plan outlined by the Obama administration last year.

Some of these religious organizations, including some Catholic and other Christian groups, have also brought suits against the government mandate. Those are still being adjudicated in lower courts.

How Does This Federal Case Relate to State Laws Governing Contraception Coverage?

More than half the states have their own laws mandating contraception coverage, and most of them have some sort of exemption for religious employers. One key difference between the federal law and state laws is that under the federal health law, employers offering non-grandfathered health coverage must provide contraceptives without cost-sharing to female employees.

What Does the Ruling Mean for Employers?

Some analysts who agreed with the Obama administration think the ruling means that employers could use religious objections to opt out of other areas of health care coverage. For example, earlier this month Barry Lynn, executive director of Americans United for Separation of Church and State, told KHN that in health care alone, "Scientology-believing employers could insist upon non-coverage of its nemesis, psychiatry. And Jehovah's Witnesses' corporations could demand exclusion of surgical coverage, under the theory that so many of such procedures require the use of whole blood products, forbidden by their faith."

But Justice Alito's decision went to lengths to limit the scope of the decision. "This decision concerns only the contraceptive mandate and should not be understood to hold that all insurance-coverage mandates, e.g. for vaccinations or blood transfusions, must necessarily fall if they conflict with an employer's religious beliefs."

The Misconceptions About Planned Parenthood Are Intentional

Dayna Evans

In the following viewpoint, Dayna Evans details the nine most common misconceptions about Planned Parenthood. Founded in 1916 in New York City, Planned Parenthood is a nonprofit organization that provides reproductive health care in the United States. Not only that, but Planned Parenthood has also supported reproductive health efforts around the world. For years, Planned Parenthood and other family planning organizations have been under assault in the media, even by President Donald Trump and Vice President Mike Pence, who do not believe that women should be allowed to choose for themselves whether an abortion is right for them. Evans is a writer and editor for New York *magazine's the Cut.*

As you read, consider the following questions:

1. Other than seeking an abortion, what are the reasons why one in five women will visit a Planned Parenthood in her lifetime?
2. Per the viewpoint, what is the most popular service provided by Planned Parenthood? Why is it important for women to have this access?
3. Does having access to reproductive education encourage teenagers to have more sex? Why or why not?

"9 Things People Get Wrong About Planned Parenthood," by Dayna Evans, *New York* Media LLC, January 5, 2017.

D o you know what Planned Parenthood actually does? If you believe Donald Trump and Mike Pence, it's an "abortion factory." If you listen to Carly Fiorina, it's a place where body parts are trafficked. While one in five women will visit a Planned Parenthood in her lifetime, terminating a pregnancy is hardly the only reason why. Nonetheless, the fact that abortion accounts for such a small part of the organization's services does little to distill egregious conservative fantasies about the right to choose.

The many misconceptions about Planned Parenthood empower the long assault against reproductive rights, and with the president-elect's promise to cut the 100-year-old health-care provider's federal funding, correcting those myths and bolstering supporters with valuable information is more important than ever. Not sure about what Planned Parenthood does and doesn't do (ahem: wholesale fetal tissue)? Here's a handy guide to nine things people get wrong about our nation's biggest women's-health-care provider.

FALSE: Abortion is the most popular service that Planned Parenthood provides.

Though some pro-lifers paint Planned Parenthood as an organization that exists for the sole purpose of blithely doling out abortions to all who walk through their doors, abortion accounts for only 3 percent of the organization's health-care services (a statistic that conservatives claim distracts from the actual cost of abortion). The main reasons people visit a Planned Parenthood are contraceptive access (31 percent) and STI/STD testing and treatment (45 percent). More than double the number of people visited Planned Parenthood clinics in 2014 for pregnancy tests than for abortion procedures.

FALSE: Planned Parenthood only provides services to women.

If Planned Parenthood were to be defunded, women won't be the only ones to lose out. While services vary depending on location, men can visit clinics for prostate, colon, and testicular cancer screenings, vasectomies, male infertility screenings, and sexual-health services, among other necessary health treatments. In 2014, Planned Parenthoods nationwide provided vasectomies to 3,445 men.

FALSE: Planned Parenthood is just for wealthy women, so they'll find health care elsewhere if it were to be shut down.

Roughly 75 percent of Planned Parenthood's patients have income at or below 150 percent of the federal poverty level, which is one enormous reason why it is essential the organization's services not be curtailed. The federal funding that Planned Parenthood receives is largely through Medicaid reimbursements. Over half of PP facilities are in medically underserved communities, and unlike most health-care facilities, PP offers same-day appointments, longer hours, and weekend services, making access to preventive health care easier for people who work nontraditional or long hours. In total, Planned Parenthood provides 4,970,000 people worldwide with sexual and reproductive health care and education yearly.

FALSE: Defunding Planned Parenthood would be good for taxpayers.

The argument goes that if Planned Parenthood were to be cut off from federal funding, America's taxpayers would benefit. But without the necessary and low-cost health care available at PP, Medicaid spending would actually go up for the federal government and taxpayers. In low-income areas, where women depend on Planned Parenthood for Medicaid-funded contraceptive services, unwanted pregnancies would rise, which would then put a much bigger—and more long-term—burden on Medicaid spending. ThinkProgress estimated that defunding PP would cause Medicaid spending to increase by $650 million over ten years.

FALSE: Teenagers are being indoctrinated by Planned Parenthood to have sex at a young age.

One of Planned Parenthood's undersung resources is the wealth of information provided not only in clinics but online, too, at a time when sex education is critically lacking nationwide. Planned Parenthood websites receive approximately 60 million visits a year, and the organization offers both text and call options for teenagers (and adults) who are curious about sex, family planning, sexually transmitted diseases, and contraceptives. Representatives from PP assert that the clinics and information available exist as a means to educate and are not intended to encourage or push young people into anything they are not ready for. (Several studies have shown that providing young people with access to sex education is not correlated to an increase in sexual risk-taking.) Many clinics have teen advocates for other teenagers to speak to, and services offered to teens of all ages are confidential.

FALSE: Planned Parenthood is only available to cis-identifying patients.

In an effort to expand its already wide reach, Planned Parenthood now offers hormone therapy for transgender patients, a typically prohibitive or difficult-to-access medical service. While many local clinics that offer hormone-replacement therapy require letters from a patient's therapist before a prescription is given, Planned Parenthood provides HRT with "informed consent." In 26 locations of the 650 Planned Parenthoods nationwide, transgender men and women can receive testosterone or estrogen treatments. Depending on the demand, the number of clinics to provide health-care options to transgender patients is only rising.

FALSE: Planned Parenthood could survive on private donors alone.

Over 40 percent of Planned Parenthood's funding comes from federal, state, and local funds. That makes up about $553 million of Planned Parenthood's annual budget, while private donors (from its 2014–2015 report) account for only $353 million a year. Without federal funding, Planned Parenthood would have little chance of survival in communities where a large majority of patients rely on the government's Medicaid and Title X grants. Planned Parenthood's yearly expenses are upwards of $12 billion, and 82 percent of those expenses go to client services, education, and research. With half of the organization's funding cut, decisions would have to be made about which community clinics could stand the loss of services. (One current available action, the Washington Post reports, is for supporters of PP to seek medical care at Planned Parenthood to increase the number of privately insured patients at their clinics.)

FALSE: Planned Parenthood only provides services to Americans.

The fight for Planned Parenthood to stay alive may be most potent in our backyards, but it has also extended its reach globally. In 2014, Planned Parenthood Global distributed sexual and reproductive health resources and information to 1,033,964 people worldwide by providing grants to local organizations in countries where access to these resources is severely limited.

FALSE: There will be thousands of other clinics available to women should Planned Parenthood be defunded.

While Planned Parenthood is certainly the most recognizable and most familiar abortion provider to most American women, it surely cannot be the only place where women can get an abortion, should they choose to, right? Right? Not so. The argument goes that if PP lost federal funding, local community health centers could step up to fight the good fight and provide health-care services in its stead. But local community centers do not have the bandwidth to take on the Medicaid- and Medicare-supported patients who depend on access to PP's availability of resources. A study by the

Guttmacher Institute found that in the 491 counties where there are currently Planned Parenthood clinics, 103 of them have no other clinics where low-income patients can gain access to affordable contraceptive services, should PP's services be drained.

In the United States Maternal Mortality Is Shockingly High

Nina Martin and Renee Montagne

In the following excerpted viewpoint, Nina Martin and Renee Montagne share the story of Lauren Bloomstein, a thirty-three-year-old nurse from Texas who died shortly after giving birth at nearly forty weeks. Bloomstein's death from preeclampsia was one of many that could have been prevented had the medical staff treating her paid closer attention to her vitals post-partum. Bloomstein is one of the seven hundred to nine hundred women in the United States who dies from pregnancy or other childbirth-related causes, the worst record in the developed world. Additionally women are often unprepared for life in the weeks after childbirth and are released from the hospital with little information about how to handle the changes in their body and the recovery. Martin covers sex and gender issues for ProPublica. Montagne is special correspondent and host for NPR News at National Public Radio.

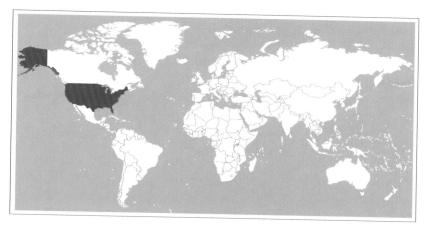

As you read, consider the following questions:

1. Why are pregnancies in the United States so high risk for women, especially women of color and low-income women?

2. Drawing from the viewpoint, why are women not monitored as closely as their children following childbirth?

3. Why are life-saving practices for mothers occurring more often in some states in the United States, rather than others? How can this be changed?

As a neonatal intensive care nurse, Lauren Bloomstein had been taking care of other people's babies for years. Finally, at 33, she was expecting one of her own. The prospect of becoming a mother made her giddy, her husband, Larry, recalled recently—"the happiest and most alive I'd ever seen her."

When Lauren was 13, her own mother had died of a massive heart attack. Lauren had lived with her older brother for a while, then with a neighbor in Hazlet, N.J., who was like a surrogate mom, but in important ways she'd grown up mostly alone. The chance to create her own family, to be the mother she didn't have, touched a place deep inside her.

"All she wanted to do was be loved," said Frankie Hedges, who took Lauren in as a teenager and thought of her as her daughter. "I think everybody loved her, but nobody loved her the way she wanted to be loved."

Other than some nausea in her first trimester, the pregnancy went smoothly. Lauren was "tired in the beginning, achy in the end," said Jackie Ennis, her best friend since high school, who talked to her at least once a day. "She gained what she's supposed to. She looked great, she felt good, she worked as much as she could"—at least three, 12-hour shifts a week until late into her ninth month. Larry, a doctor, helped monitor her blood pressure at home, and all was normal.

On her days off she got organized, picking out strollers and car seats, stocking up on diapers and onesies. After one last pre-baby vacation to the Caribbean, she and Larry went hunting for their forever home, settling on a brick colonial with black shutters and a big yard in Moorestown, N.J., not far from his new job as an orthopedic trauma surgeon in Camden. Lauren wanted the baby's gender to be a surprise, so when she set up the nursery she left the walls unpainted—she figured she'd have plenty of time to choose colors later. Despite all she knew about what could go wrong, she seemed untroubled by the normal expectant-mom anxieties. Her only real worry was going into labor prematurely. "You have to stay in there at least until 32 weeks," she would tell her belly. "I see how the babies do before 32. Just don't come out too soon."

When she reached 39 weeks and six days—Friday, Sept. 30, 2011—Larry and Lauren drove to Monmouth Medical Center in Long Branch, the hospital where the two of them had met in 2004 and where she'd spent virtually her entire career. If anyone would watch out for her and her baby, Lauren figured, it would be the doctors and nurses she worked with on a daily basis. She was especially fond of her obstetrician/gynecologist, who had trained as a resident at Monmouth at the same time as Larry. Lauren wasn't having contractions, but she and the ob/gyn agreed to schedule an induction of labor—he was on call that weekend and would be sure to handle the delivery himself.

Inductions often go slowly, and Lauren's labor stretched well into the next day. Ennis talked to her on the phone several times: "She said she was feeling OK, she was just really uncomfortable." At one point, Lauren was overcome by a sudden, sharp pain in her back near her kidneys or liver, but the nurses bumped up her epidural and the stabbing stopped.

Inductions have been associated with higher cesarean-section rates, but Lauren progressed well enough to deliver vaginally. On Saturday, Oct. 1, at 6:49 p.m., 23 hours after she checked into the hospital, Hailey Anne Bloomstein was born, weighing 5 pounds, 12 ounces. Larry and Lauren's family had been camped out in the waiting room; now they swarmed into the delivery area to ooh and aah, marveling at how Lauren seemed to glow.

Larry floated around on his own cloud of euphoria, phone camera in hand. In one 35-second video, Lauren holds their daughter on her chest, stroking her cheek with a practiced touch. Hailey is bundled in hospital-issued pastels and flannel, unusually alert for a newborn; she studies her mother's face as if trying to make sense of a mystery that will never be solved. The delivery room staff bustles in the background in the low-key way of people who believe everything has gone exactly as it's supposed to.

Then Lauren looks directly at the camera, her eyes brimming. Twenty hours later, she was dead.

"We don't pay enough attention"

The ability to protect the health of mothers and babies in childbirth is a basic measure of a society's development. Yet every year in the U.S., 700 to 900 women die from pregnancy or childbirth-related causes, and some 65,000 nearly die—by many measures, the worst record in the developed world.

American women are more than three times as likely as Canadian women to die in the maternal period (defined by the

African American Maternal Mortality

You live in a country with the highest per capita income in the world, more people have health insurance than ever before in your nation's history, you're surrounded by some of the best medical facilities in the world, and women are dying in childbirth at rates on par with countries that have vastly fewer national resources and medical infrastructure.

Welcome to the United States. For the last two decades, maternal mortality rates have risen sharply in the U.S.–even amid Americans' expanded access to health care through the Affordable Care Act. For Black women, maternal mortality rates have reached critical levels, with Black women dying from pregnancy-related complications at 3.5 times the rate of their white counterparts nationally. In Texas, Black women make up roughly 11 percent of the state's births but almost a third of the mothers who die in childbirth.

A lack of access to quality and affordable health care certainly plays a role, as do overlapping health disparities. But for communities of color, and Black communities in particular, those factors are compounded with discrimination and implicit racial bias in medical treatment that can lead to pregnant Black women receiving different and often worse care. This can lead to further complications and greatly increase their risk of maternal death. The maternal mortality rate for Black women in the U.S. cuts across age, education, and income level–a terrifying reality in a country as well-resourced as the U.S.

So when politicians propose six and 20-week abortion bans and threaten birth control access while salivating over the opportunity to repeal the Affordable Care Act, "defund" Planned Parenthood, and close health centers that serve pregnant and parenting moms, excuse us if we call foul on their disingenuous concern for women's lives. True care for women and families means providing access to quality, compassionate, and affordable health care, like you get at Planned Parenthood, not eliminating health centers that provide it. It also means ensuring women, their families, and their communities have access to all of the "social supports in safe environments and healthy communities, and without fear of violence from individuals or the government."

"We need to talk about the maternal mortality rate for Black women in the U.S." by Samantha Master, Planned Parenthood Action Fund, Inc, November 3, 2017.

Centers for Disease Control as the start of pregnancy to one year after delivery or termination), six times as likely to die as Scandinavians. In every other wealthy country, and many less affluent ones, maternal mortality rates have been falling; in Great Britain, the journal Lancet recently noted, the rate has declined so dramatically that "a man is more likely to die while his partner is pregnant than she is." But in the U.S., maternal deaths increased from 2000 to 2014. In a recent analysis by the CDC Foundation, nearly 60 percent of such deaths are preventable.

While maternal mortality is significantly more common among African-Americans, low-income women and in rural areas, pregnancy and childbirth complications kill women of every race and ethnicity, education and income level, in every part of the U.S. ProPublica and NPR spent the last several months scouring social media and other sources, ultimately identifying more than 450 expectant and new mothers who have died since 2011.

The list includes teachers, insurance brokers, homeless women, journalists, a spokeswoman for Yellowstone National Park, a co-founder of the YouTube channel WhatsUpMoms, and more than a dozen doctors and nurses like Lauren Bloomstein. They died from cardiomyopathy and other heart problems, massive hemorrhage, blood clots, infections and pregnancy-induced hypertension (preeclampsia) as well as rarer causes. Many died days or weeks after leaving the hospital. Maternal mortality is commonplace enough that three new mothers who died, including Lauren, were cared for by the same ob/gyn.

The reasons for higher maternal mortality in the U.S. are manifold. New mothers are older than they used to be, with more complex medical histories. Half of pregnancies in the U.S. are unplanned, so many women don't address chronic health issues beforehand. Greater prevalence of C-sections leads to more life-threatening complications. The fragmented health system makes it harder for new mothers, especially those without good insurance, to get the care they need. Confusion about how to recognize worrisome symptoms and treat obstetric emergencies makes caregivers more prone to error.

Yet the worsening U.S. maternal mortality numbers contrast sharply with the impressive progress in saving babies' lives. Infant mortality has fallen to its lowest point in history, the CDC reports, reflecting 50 years of efforts by the public health community to prevent birth defects, reduce preterm birth, and improve outcomes for very premature infants. The number of babies who die annually in the U.S.—about 23,000 in 2014—still greatly exceeds the number of expectant and new mothers who die, but the ratio is narrowing.

[...]

In regular maternity wards, too, babies are monitored more closely than mothers during and after birth, maternal health advocates told ProPublica and NPR. Newborns in the slightest danger are whisked off to neonatal intensive care units like the one Lauren Bloomstein worked at, staffed by highly trained specialists ready for the worst, while their mothers are tended by nurses and doctors who expect things to be fine and are often unprepared when they aren't.

When women are discharged, they routinely receive information about how to breast-feed and what to do if their newborn is sick but not necessarily how to tell if they need medical attention themselves. "It was only when I had my own child that I realized, 'Oh my goodness. That was completely insufficient information,'" said Elizabeth Howell, professor of obstetrics and gynecology at the Icahn School of Medicine at Mount Sinai Hospital in New York City.

"The way that we've been trained, we do not give women enough information for them to manage their health postpartum. The focus had always been on babies and not on mothers."

In 2009, the Joint Commission, which accredits 21,000 health care facilities in the U.S., adopted a series of perinatal "core measures"—national standards that have been shown to reduce complications and improve patient outcomes. Four of the measures are aimed at making sure the baby is healthy. One—bringing down the C-section rate—addresses maternal health.

Meanwhile, life-saving practices that have become widely accepted in other affluent countries—and in a few states, notably California—have yet to take hold in many American hospitals. Take the example of preeclampsia, a type of high blood pressure that occurs only in pregnancy or the postpartum period, and can lead to seizures and strokes. Around the world, it kills an estimated five women an hour. But in developed countries, it is highly treatable. The key is to act quickly.

By standardizing its approach, Britain has reduced preeclampsia deaths to one in a million—a total of two deaths from 2012 to 2014. In the U.S., on the other hand, preeclampsia still accounts for about 8 percent of maternal deaths—50 to 70 women a year. Including Lauren Bloomstein.

[…]

"I don't feel good"

Larry Bloomstein's first inkling that something was seriously wrong with Lauren came about 90 minutes after she gave birth. He had accompanied Hailey up to the nursery to be weighed and measured and given the usual barrage of tests for newborns. Lauren hadn't eaten since breakfast, but he returned to find her dinner tray untouched. "I don't feel good," she told him. She pointed to a spot above her abdomen and just below her sternum, close to where she'd felt the stabbing sensation during labor. "I've got pain that's coming back."

Larry had been at Lauren's side much of the previous 24 hours. Conscious that his role was husband rather than doctor, he had tried not to overstep. Now, though, he pressed Vaclavik: What was the matter with his wife? "He was like, 'I see this a lot. We do a lot of belly surgery. This is definitely reflux,'" Larry recalled. According to Lauren's records, the ob/gyn ordered an antacid called Bicitra and an opioid painkiller called Dilaudid. Lauren vomited them up.

Lauren's pain was soon 10 on a scale of 10, she told Larry and the nurses; so excruciating, the nurses noted, "Patient [is] unable to stay still." Just as ominously, her blood pressure was spiking. An hour after Hailey's birth, the reading was 160/95; an hour after that, 169/108. At her final prenatal appointment, her reading had been just 118/69. Obstetrics wasn't Larry's specialty, but he knew enough to ask the nurse: Could this be preeclampsia?

Preeclampsia, or pregnancy-related hypertension, is a little-understood condition that affects 3 percent to 5 percent of expectant or new mothers in the U.S., up to 200,000 women a year. It can strike anyone out of the blue, though the risk is higher for African-Americans, women with pre-existing conditions such as obesity, diabetes or kidney disease, and mothers over the age of 40. It is most common during the second half of pregnancy, but can develop in the days or weeks after childbirth, and can become very dangerous very quickly. Because a traditional treatment for preeclampsia is to deliver as soon as possible, the babies are often premature and end up in NICUs like the one where Lauren worked.

As Larry suspected, Lauren's blood pressure readings were well past the danger point. What he didn't know was that they'd been abnormally high since she entered the hospital—147/99, according to her admissions paperwork. During labor, she had 21 systolic readings at or above 140 and 13 diastolic readings at or above 90, her records indicated; for a stretch of almost eight hours, her blood pressure wasn't monitored at all, the New Jersey Department of Health later found. Over that same period, her baby's vital signs were being constantly watched, Larry said.

In his court deposition, Vaclavik described the 147/99 reading as "elevated" compared to her usual readings, but not abnormal. He "would use 180 over 110 as a cutoff" to suspect preeclampsia, he said. Still, he acknowledged, Lauren's blood pressure "might have been recommended to be monitored more closely, in retrospect."

Leading medical organizations in the U.S. and the U.K. take a different view. They advise that increases to 140/90 for pregnant women with no previous history of high blood pressure signify preeclampsia. When systolic readings hit 160, treatment with anti-hypertensive drugs and magnesium sulfate to prevent seizures "should be initiated ASAP," according to guidelines from the Alliance for Innovation on Maternal Health.

When other symptoms, such as upper abdominal (epigastric) pain, are present, the situation is considered even more urgent.

This basic approach isn't new: "Core Curriculum for Maternal-Newborn Nursing," a widely used textbook, outlined it in 1997. Yet failure to diagnose preeclampsia, or to differentiate it from chronic high blood pressure, is all too common.

California researchers who studied preeclampsia deaths over several years found one striking theme: "Despite triggers that clearly indicated a serious deterioration in the patient's condition, health care providers failed to recognize and respond to these signs in a timely manner, leading to delays in diagnosis and treatment."

[...]

American Men Have No Reproductive Rights

Michael Bargo Jr.

In the following viewpoint, Michael Bargo Jr. posits that there is a significant lack of reproductive protections for men in the United States. Bargo claims that the debate has become incredibly one-sided in favor of women, and he also details the perceived stereotypes regarding women being considered more nurturing and better parents than men. In this viewpoint, the author states that there is very little incentive to change these laws to make them more equal and to give men more rights for things like to have a child or to see a child when there is no relationship between the parents, whether in the present or past. Bargo is a writer and photographer who has published many articles on American Thinker on Illinois politics.

As you read, consider the following questions:

1. Do there need to be laws to protect men's reproductive rights? If so, what would these laws be?
2. Do women really get a "free ride" with sex, as the author of the viewpoint posits? Why or why not?
3. Should a man be able to sue a woman for, as the author of the viewpoint claims, "depriving him of a child"? Why or why not?

"American Men Have No Reproductive Rights," by Michael Bargo, Jr., American Thinker, August 10, 2015. Reprinted by permission.

The debate and policy initiatives to establish and codify reproductive rights for women are sexist and reflect gender bias. There are few, if any, laws and policies in the U.S. at the state or Federal levels which make any effort to protect men regarding their reproductive rights. The debate has been so one-sided that most people don't even think about this as an issue, yet a quick review of the topic reveals the extent to which men's reproductive rights have been not just ignored but aggressively impaired. In Marxist terms, men as a class are engaged in an historic struggle to establish their rights.

Here are some examples. Right now many states have family laws which clearly establish that when a man engages in the sex act with a woman, he is, by virtue of willfully participating in that act, agreeing to an irrevocable, binding legal contract to support the child financially if the woman becomes pregnant. But women are allowed a free ride on the sex act. There is no law in Illinois, or I would venture to say, any other state that stipulates that a woman who willfully engages in the sex act with a man thereby enters into a binding contractual agreement to allow the man to visit the child created by the act and have an unlimited opportunity to text or email the child 24/7 throughout the life of the child.

These issues, of men's rights in child custody are largely ignored by law. They are left to be resolved by divorce courts, which are stuck in the past with regard to sexual stereotyping and gender bias. And it is a situation women are loath to change. There is no incentive for them to change. After all, as things stand now, women have all the reproductive rights and men are left only with the responsibilities. They are fighting an uphill battle in court when they seek to assert their rights as a biological father.

A woman is not likely go to jail for refusing to allow the father of the children to see them on visitation days. And there are no punishments for women who direct hateful speech regarding their ex-husband to their children.

Noted family lawyer Jeff Leving was able, after a great deal of effort, to pass a father's visitation rights law in Illinois. But his is hard to enforce and it is a constant battle.

Similarly, men have no reproductive rights with regard to saving the life of their child from abortion. The plain fact is if a woman becomes pregnant the right to abort is hers alone. The man involved, even the husband, has no legally enforceable right to prevent the abortion. This is particularly painful for men who, during courtship, told their fiancé they wanted to have a family.

While the nation and the Supreme Court are engaged in a serious debate of same-sex marriage rights, the right of traditional husbands are largely left ignored. These issues are difficult to enforce through litigation and after an abortion has been performed there is no remedy. A man cannot sue his wife for depriving him of a child. Even if he attempted to do so it would be very difficult to win that kind of case.

Which brings up another set of gender stereotypes and institutionalized sexism. The prejudices against men's reproductive rights are ancient and deep. While feminist activists have repeated, and continue to repeat, that women cannot be victimized by old gender stereotypes, few if any media commentators discuss the idea that men are victimized by stereotypes. To this day the stereotypes are repeated that men only want sex from women.

Our society is not encouraged to overcome the stereotypes that ridicule men. This may be part of a strategy. Those who wish to put down men with old-fashioned stereotypes, such as that men only want women for one thing and will readily engage in the sex act with any stranger, may be putting men down just so they will lose children in divorce court and have to pay. This brings up an interesting point: while the nation is encouraged to dismiss stereotypes about women, such as that they cannot make responsible decisions or hold demanding executive jobs, when it comes to reproductive rights the stereotypes that men can't control their sexual impulses and that they should have to pay for everything are stereotypes that are reinforced and perpetrated with glee.

The stereotypes against men merely serve to deprive them of reproductive rights. Women are not naturally better at nurturing, we are told. This stereotype is refuted to support the idea that there is no reason that married men can't help take care of the kids. But judges usually think children are better off with their mothers. Unless, of course, the man who wants custody is in a same-sex marriage and wants to adopt. Then, somehow, a nurturing male is a possibility that should be seriously defended.

Another major stereotype that interferes with men's reproductive rights is that men are naturally violent. This enables judges to quickly approve of "temporary restraining orders" and "orders of protection" against husbands. All the wife has to do is allege in court that she is "afraid" that the husband may strike her. And this TRO is granted even if the husband has absolutely no history of violence.

These three stereotypes, that 1) men don't want to take care of children and are only interested in sex, 2) that men are defined by society as the wage earners, and 3) that men are naturally prone to domestic violence, are used by women and their lawyers to continue the abuse of fathers and deprive them of the affection of their children. In brief, men are selfish, violent, uncaring brutes naturally unfit to be fathers. How convenient to the family court system, and to women who want custody and the house.

And women complain that they alone have to battle against stereotypes. The anti-father stereotypes don't matter as long as the stereotypes are used to get custody of the children, monthly child support, alimony checks, and the house to the ex-wife.

When these issues are combined they reveal how men's reproductive rights can be denied every day in family courts, how the legal system disrespects the rights of fathers, and how children are used by women and their lawyers as pawns in a system designed to break apart families and disrupt the emotional bond between fathers and their children. A system designed to make fathers angry, to create great emotional distress to the children, and ruin the family the father wanted to have and care for.

These stereotypes have political ramifications as well. Aristotle wrote that the fundamental political unit is the family. Democrats have taken this idea and convinced women, through the use of anti-male stereotypes, that only the State, in particular their Party, can protect the rights of women from men. All women have to do is vote for them.

Reproductive Coercion Is a Form of Sexual Assault

Kat Stoeffel

In the following viewpoint, Kat Stoeffel tells the stories of women who keep getting pregnant, even though they make the effort to delay pregnancy. According to the American College of Obstetrics and Gynecologists (ACOG), it is recommended that OB-GYNS screen their patients and their partners for reproductive coercion, including poking holes in condoms, hiding birth control pills, or even threats to leave or of personal harm if they do not get pregnant. The ACOG classes reproductive coercion as a form of sexual assault, carried out by male abusers who want to exercise control over their partner's bodies. One of the unique aspects of this form of abuse is that women by and large are unaware that reproductive coercion is a form of sexual assault and abuse.

As you read, consider the following questions:

1. In what ways is reproductive coercion a form of sexual assault?
2. Why does domestic violence disproportionately affect low-income women?
3. Drawing from your answer to the previous question, is reproductive coercion a classed issue? Why or why not?

L indsay Clark, M.D., couldn't figure out why her patients were getting pregnant. An obstetrics and gynecology resident in Rhode Island, she was treating women who very recently had been pregnant, or had come to her with the opposite intent. "I wondered why women were getting pregnant so soon after they came to me for birth control counseling," she told the Cut. "I became interested in the idea that women might not have as much control over their birth control as they think."

Surveying 641 women who received routine ob-gyn care at Providence's Women and Infants Hospital, Clark found that 16 percent had received unwelcome pressure to get pregnant. Their boyfriends and partners made it hard for them to use birth control—poking holes in condoms or hiding their pills—or threatened to leave or harm them if they didn't get pregnant.

If you don't hear much these days about the stereotypical gold digger who lies about being on the pill to ensnare a man into marriage or eighteen years of child support payments, that may be because doctors are now being told to look for just the opposite: The woman whose partner sabotages her birth control. She's not so hard to find.

Early this year, the American College of Obstetrics and Gynecologists (ACOG) issued a committee recommendation urging ob-gyns to screen patients for these behaviors, collectively known as reproductive coercion. Whether women were in for an annual exam, a pregnancy test, or a second trimester visit, it recommended asking questions like, "Does your partner support your decision about when or if you want to become pregnant?"

The ACOG's strategy reflects a growing body of research that identifies reproductive coercion as a unique form of domestic or intimate partner violence, and offers an explanation for the high rates of unintended pregnancies among women in abusive relationships. Increasingly, birth-control sabotage is viewed as a tool not for baby-crazed female stalkers, but for a class of predominantly male abusers who want to exercise control over their partner's body, make her dependent upon them, or secure a long-term presence in her life.

One of the subject's leading experts, the Children's Hospital of Pittsburgh's chief of adolescent medicine Elizabeth E. Miller, M.D., Ph.D., began looking into the phenomenon less than a decade ago, after seeing a 15-year-old patient who said her boyfriend only used condoms some of the time. Rather than asking whether the boyfriend refused her request to use condoms, she assumed the patient needed to be educated about birth control. Two weeks later, the girl was in the emergency room with a severe head injury. "Personally, it was incredibly destabilizing," Miller recalled. "It was like, 'How could I have missed this?'" Later, she interviewed girls who were known to have been in violent relationships for a 2007 paper on the topic. "A quarter of them said, 'He was trying to get me pregnant.'"

In Miller's 2010 study, one of the largest on reproductive coercion to date, 15 percent of 1,300 women who visited federal- and state-subsidized California family-planning clinics had their birth control sabotaged. One in five had been urged by a boyfriend not to use birth control, or told by a boyfriend he would leave her if she wouldn't get pregnant. A larger portion of respondents, 35 percent, who reported intimate partner violence (IPV) also reported birth-control sabotage.

Because Miller's study examined low-income-friendly clinics —and because domestic violence disproportionately affects low-income women—some have conjectured that reproductive coercion is a classed issue. But Dr. Clark's survey, which looked at a general population of patients, with and without private insurance, suggests birth-control sabotage and pregnancy coercion happen at a similar rate across socioeconomic and educational backgrounds. In her study, the single highest risk factor for reproductive coercion was being unmarried and sexually active.

Miller's co-author Rebecca Levenson, a senior policy analyst for Futures Without Violence, said she expects more and diverse women will come forward as information about reproductive coercion spreads and women recognize it as a kind of abuse. "Naming something is powerful," she said. But first, she hopes the research will inform the many doctors who are in a position to directly intervene and reduce the reproductive harm facing IPV victims—be it an unwanted pregnancy, an expensive abortion, or the unhappy extension of a bad relationship — but don't know to ask. Harm-reduction strategies range from offering birth control or emergency contraceptives in plain packaging to switching women to a stealthier method, like Depo Provera hormone shots or an IUD with the strings clipped.

Levenson described a 17-year-old she interviewed whose boyfriend claimed the condom broke six times in a row before she sought out Depo Provera for herself. This was before reproductive coercion was widely discussed, she said, but "Imagine how powerful it would be if when she went to the clinic the clinician would say, 'Hey, you've come in for emergency contraceptive three times. Are you at all worried about that?'"

When Futures Without Violence took their findings to Eve Espey, M.D., M.P.H., a professor of obstetrics and gynecology at the University of New Mexico and an author of the ACOG's committee opinion, she was "totally embarrassed," she said. "I've always asked patients about intimate partner violence, but I had not asked specifically about reproductive coercion," she told the Cut. "I was amazed that a seasoned ob-gyn like I am was not aware of that as an entity."

Once she became aware, she wasn't surprised how common it was among her patients. In addition to the IUD and the shot, in some cases Espey recommends patients switch to a non-hormonal IUD because "there are some men who count the days of women's periods," which can be fewer if she's on hormonal birth control. "When people have power and control needs, they will seek the information," she explained.

Citing the high rate of response to her survey, Dr. Clark told the Cut that patients are equally quick to identify reproductive coercion once aware of its existence. "In my practice, they say, 'Oh, I've never really thought about it like that, but, yeah, I do get pressure,'" she said. "Women want to talk about it." Finally, they will have someone with whom they can.

Periodical and Internet Sources Bibliography

The following articles have been selected to supplement the diverse views presented in this chapter.

Gary Barker and Serra Sippel, "What do Men have to do with Women's Reproductive Rights?" Girls Globe, August 10, 2017. https://www.girlsglobe.org/2017/08/10/womens-reproductive-rights-men/.

Alia E. Dastagir, "What do men get that women don't? Here are a few things," *USA Today*, March 23, 2017. https://www.usatoday.com/story/news/2017/03/01/2017-womens-history-month/98247518/.

Eliana Dockterman, "5 Things Women Need to Know About the Hobby Lobby Ruling," *Time*, July 1, 2014. http://time.com/2941323/supreme-court-contraception-ruling-hobby-lobby/.

Debra Goldschmidt and Ashley Strickland, "Planned Parenthood: Fast facts and revealing numbers," CNN, August 1, 2017. https://www.cnn.com/2015/08/04/health/planned-parenthood-by-the-numbers/index.html.

Sonja Haller, "Finally! In 2018 it's legal to breastfeed in public in all 50 states," *USA Today*, July 25, 2018. https://www.usatoday.com/story/life/allthemoms/2018/07/25/public-breastfeeding-now-legal-all-50-states/835372002/.

Jessie Hellman, "Maternal deaths keep rising in US, raising scrutiny," The Hill, April 19, 2018. https://thehill.com/policy/healthcare/383847-lawmakers-pressed-to-act-as-us-struggles-with-maternal-deaths.

Yuanyuan Kelly, "6 myths about Planned Parenthood in the United States," Global Citizen, August 7, 2015. https://www.globalcitizen.org/en/content/6-myths-about-planned-parenthood/.

Marian F. MacDorman, Eugene Declercq, Howard Cabral, Christine Morton, "Is the United States Maternal Mortality Rate Increasing? Disentangling trends from measurement issues Short title: U.S. Maternal Mortality Trends," US National Library of

Medicine National Institutes of Health, September 2016. https://www.ncbi.nlm.nih.gov/pmc/articles/PMC5001799/.

Amanda Marcotte, "'Hobby Lobby' Is About Blocking Contraception Access, Not Religious Liberty," Rewire News, July 15, 2015. https://rewire.news/article/2015/07/15/hobby-lobby-blocking-contraception-access-religious-liberty/.

Heather Marcoux, "Breastfeeding in public is natural—and legally protected," Motherly, July 19, 2018. https://www.mother.ly/news/breastfeeding-in-public-is-legally-protected.

Tracy Moore, "The Men's Guide to the War on Reproductive Rights," Mel Magazine, June 2018. https://melmagazine.com/en-us/story/the-mens-guide-to-the-war-on-reproductive-rights.

Jay Newton-Small, "How Women Secretly Won the Hobby Lobby Fight," Time, January 6, 2016. http://time.com/4168895/hobby-lobby-women-congress-white-house/.

USA Today Editorial Board, "High maternal death rate shames America among developed nations," USA Today, July 31, 2018. https://www.usatoday.com/story/opinion/2018/07/31/high-maternal-death-rate-shames-america-developed-nations-editorials-debates/866752002/.

Miriam Wasser, "Top 10 Myths About Planned Parenthood," Phoenix New Times, September 17, 2015. https://www.phoenixnewtimes.com/news/top-10-myths-about-planned-parenthood-7654346.

GLOBALVIEWPOINTS

CHAPTER 3

Reproductive Rights and Religion

In the United States Crisis Pregnancy Centers Are Challenging the Reproductive FACT Act

Linley Sanders

In the following viewpoint, Linley Sanders details the reasons why the National Institute of Family and Life Advocates (NIFLA) is challenging California State Law AB 775, also known as the Reproductive FACT Act. This law required health centers in California to inform women about low-cost, public programs for family planning, including both birth control and abortion. The NIFLA is challenging the law because it believes it stifles the free speech of faith-based organizations that do not believe a woman should have the ability to seek out an abortion in a safe and sanitary environment and should be encouraged to carry the pregnancy to term, whether she wants to have a child or not. Sanders is a data journalist with a focus on women's political interests and a contributing news reporter for TeenVogue.com.

As you read, consider the following questions:

1. Should it be legal for crisis pregnancy centers to provide inaccurate information to women seeking abortions? Why or why not?

2. Does the First Amendment protect organizations from providing accurate, fact-based information to women regarding their health? Why or why not?

3. How many states mandate that women must be given antiabortion counseling prior to undergoing the procedure, and why is it important that women be given all the facts prior to making a decision?

After Lauren Gray learned, at her small-town college, that she was pregnant, she sought out a women's health center clinic near her campus and asked to hear her options regarding an abortion. The woman helping her at the crisis pregnancy center, she said, explained that the clinic was actually pro-life, and therefore, she would be able to hear only about adoption resources or options for keeping the baby.

Lauren said she left the clinic confused and eventually received an abortion, according to the Associated Press. Now 28, Lauren speaks out against crisis pregnancy centers, which are organizations, often religiously based, designed to deter women from pursuing abortions—often by hiding it as an option or providing inaccurate information. Lauren told Teen Vogue over email as she traveled to an abortion-rights rally in Washington D.C., that "even when you do your homework," the anti-abortion crisis pregnancy centers often appear reputable.

"There are so many risks for young women, and when you are in vulnerable situations and having to make critical a decision about your reproductive health care—which can be really scary and hard—it's especially critical to get the full, accurate information you need to make the most informed, best decision," Lauren told Teen Vogue. "But instead, these fake clinics delay care in the case of abortion, which is not in the interest of any young woman trying to make an informed decision, especially one where timing is so important."

In a Supreme Court case that is scheduled for arguments today, March 20, a legal resource for crisis pregnancy centers called the National Institute of Family and Life Advocates (NIFLA) is challenging California state law AB 775, aka the Reproductive FACT Act. The law requires licensed health care centers in California to inform women about low-cost, public programs for family planning—including birth control and abortion. This is what you need to know as the Supreme Court considers the case.

Why is NIFLA challenging the law?

NIFLA provides legal counsel to anti-abortion pregnancy centers and medical clinics. It is challenging the California law on behalf of anti-abortion pregnancy centers, which do not want to provide information about the state's low-cost programs for birth control or abortions because it represents a "violation of their conscience," according to the NIFLA response submitted to the Supreme Court.

People opposed to the law are unhappy with an exemption for women's health clinics that enroll people in public programs—essentially, programs that support abortion rights, according to an amicus brief. NIFLA argues that the law violates the clinics' First

Amendment right to free speech and if permitted, would "radically empower the government to control speech" and "lessen speech protections" for religious organizations and advocacy nonprofits.

Why is California defending the FACT Act?

More than 700,000 women in California become pregnant each year, and one-half of these pregnancies are unintended, according to data provided in the Reproductive FACT Act. In order to ensure women quickly receive accurate information about their pregnancy options, the California Legislature required unlicensed facilities offering pregnancy tests to disclose that they were not actual medical facilities and to publicly provide information about prenatal care, contraception, and abortion services.

California's Attorney General Xavier Becerra has argued in his Supreme Court brief that the law does not violate the free speech section of the First Amendment, but rather enables women to "secure the services they deem appropriate."

What have lower courts decided?

According to NBC News, two lower courts that reviewed the case both agreed with California's argument. Each court maintained that the state is permitted to ensure that its citizens are provided the full scope of medical information.

What is at stake in the case?

According to NARAL Pro-Choice America, if crisis pregnancy centers are allowed to deceive patients or lie about medical facts, then more women like Lauren will risk getting tricked or delayed in seeking an abortion.

If the Supreme Court agrees with NIFLA, there could also be a setback to the anti-abortion movement. According to the pro-choice Guttmacher Institute, 18 states mandate that women are given anti-abortion counseling before undergoing the medical procedure. A Slate analysis indicated that a ruling against California may "lead to the invalidation of anti-abortion counseling laws across the country on similar First Amendment grounds."

For Lauren, the case is more personal. She told Teen Vogue that it is a "really traumatic experience to be coerced into thinking you only have certain options." This Supreme Court case could decide if more women like her are allowed to be deceived.

"It's important because women, especially young women seeking help, deserve to know all the information and be told about every option out there," Lauren told Teen Vogue. "Women do not deserve to be lied to or made to believe they're getting advice from people who aren't even medical professionals."

How can women make their voices heard?

Lauren encourages women to start by having honest dialogues with one another about accurate medical care. If people are especially passionate about activism to help local clinics, they can work as patient escorts, but she said "having honest dialogues about this issue is extremely important" to end the power of crisis pregnancy centers in attempting to dissuade women from seeking an abortion.

"Young women should know that there's nothing to be ashamed of in seeking out your reproductive health care options," Lauren told Teen Vogue. "Just like we shouldn't be ashamed of visiting a dentist or an eye doctor."

In Islamic Countries Family Planning Programs Help Strengthen Overall Development

Babar Tasneem Shaikh, Syed Khurram Azmat, and
Arslan Mazhar

In the following excerpted viewpoint, Babar Tasneem Shaikh, Syed Khurram Azmat, and Arslan Mazhar review the advancements in family planning in Islamic countries like Pakistan, Afghanistan, Bangladesh, Egypt, Indonesia, Iran, Jordan, Kuwait, Malaysia, Morocco, Nigeria, and Turkey. They support family planning programs, including ones that educate partners on how to choose the number and timing of the births of their children. Many of these programs are important because they slow down population growth, and rapid growth rates can have a negative impact on the advancements of developing countries. Shaikh is an independent researcher. Azmat is a public health interventionist. Mazhar is a researcher with the Aga Khan Foundation in Pakistan.

"Family Planning and Contraception in Islamic Countries: A Critical Review of the Literature," by Babar Tasneem Shaikh, Syed Khurram Azmat, and Arslan Mazhar. J Pak Med Assoc. 2013;Suppl-3 Vol.63 pp S-67-S72. Reprinted by permission.

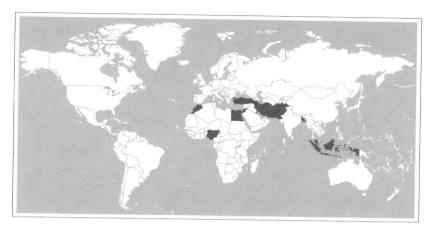

As you read, consider the following questions:

1. What are the reasons why women are unable to access family planning resources in Middle Eastern countries? How can this access be expanded?

2. In the case of Pakistan, why is it important to have lady health workers (LHWs) to assist with family planning?

3. What are the advancements made in family planning in other countries in the Middle East and Africa?

The population of the world reached seven billion in 2012. Pakistan's population stands at more than 180 million, is growing rapidly, and has the highest unmet need for family planning (FP) in isolated rural areas. The low usage of contraception in the rural areas of Pakistan correlates with the level of isolation, poverty, illiteracy, and to a large extent, religious misinterpretations/misconceptions. Almost 25% of couples who desired FP services were not receiving them for a variety of reasons of which religion could be one, especially in the rural remote areas where the media is still not reaching and influencing mind-sets. In this scenario, the role of social marketing in bringing about attitudinal and behavioural change among users in underserved areas and gatekeepers and opinion makers in society must not be neglected.

The work in promoting FP, contraception and birth spacing requires authentic evidence from similar socio-cultural contexts and this endeavour of compiling case studies from various Islamic countries on their FP initiatives is a good step. Governments around the world, including many in the Islamic world, support FP programmes to enable individuals and couples to choose the number and timing of their children.

[...]

Introduction

The introduction of modern contraceptives, the restructuring of family planning (FP) programmes, and endorsements and international agreements on birth spacing, all have given new impulses to old paradigms on the subject. In this very context, Muslims and Islamic countries have always been under debate and critique. Pakistan, for instance, is one example where the FP programme has not delivered the results desired and the common perception is that it is perhaps due to religion. This is true, to some extent. The Pakistan Demographic and Health Survey (PDHS) 2006-07 showed that six percent of women were restrained from using any FP method because of religious reasons or interpretations.[1] These interpretations and misconceptions have been propagated to declare FP a sin. The major role in this regard indubitably is of the local clergymen. Nonetheless, there are several Islamic countries that have not only presented many success stories in this regard, but have achieved control over their fertility rate and population growth rate. Governments around the world including many in the Islamic world, endorse FP programmes to facilitate individuals and couples to decide for themselves the number and timing of their children. These FP programmes have carried the slogan of improving the health of women and children besides slowing down population growth in countries where an overwhelming population growth was considered a barrier to socio-economic development. It is important to note at this juncture that most Islamic countries endorsed the Programme of Action of the United Nations 1994 International Conference on Population and Development,[2] and the 2000 Millennium Development Summit Declaration which called for universal access to FP information and services.[3] PubMed® and Google Scholar® were used as the main databases for collecting literature. This review will provide an overview of Islamic countries' policies on, and support for FP and modern contraception. For this purpose, literature from Afghanistan, Bangladesh, Egypt, Indonesia, Iran, Jordan, Kuwait, Malaysia, Morocco, Nigeria, Pakistan, and Turkey was included. This is a summary of peer-reviewed articles on Islam, contraception, and FP.

Pakistan's Context

The most common factors associated with the unmet need for FP in Pakistan include women's perceptions that their mothers-in-law have different fertility goals in mind, having less than two sons or two daughters, a lack of economic independence, a lack of spousal communication on sexual matters, and religious misinterpretations.[1] It has often been emphasized that programmes to reduce unmet need should therefore target mothers-in-law and their religious interpretations about FP because they are the main decision-makers in matters related to couples' adoption of FP, female economic independence, and encouraging spousal communication.[4] Women's autonomy has also documented some significant results in accessing FP services in areas where husbands' opposition and religious opposition are the main barriers.[5] In another study, it was documented that it is mostly religious leaders who are against FP services and that involving them proactively in community education is extremely important to promote contraception use.[6] Lady health workers (LHWs), for instance, have been found to be most effective in addressing religious myths and misconceptions with regard to FP. There is strong evidence that the LHW programme has succeeded in integrating FP into 'doorstep' provision of preventive healthcare, hence addressing the issue of women's mobility.[7] Other initiatives are direly needed to address the beliefs and perceptions of religious opinion givers about FP practices, and it is essential to develop the capacity of religious leaders in order to promote FP messages at the community level.[8] Another study states that religious leaders who had more knowledge about contraception methods actually approved of FP services. Moreover, religious leaders from more educated provinces had positive views about FP methods as compared to provinces with lower literacy rates.[9] Studying community health-seeking behaviours and conducting health systems research, of course, with religion, culture, and societal norms at their core, seems imperative in the context of Pakistan.[10]

[...]

Scenarios in Other Islamic Countries

Middle East

In Iran, decision-makers including ministry officials and religious leaders met with technical experts and collectively agreed that the country could not adequately feed, educate, house, or provide jobs to its citizens at existing levels of population growth. Faced with these facts, they took action and developed a population policy that was incorporated into the country's development plan. Family planning programmes were strengthened as a building block for poverty reduction and the achievement of national development goals.[16] Religious leaders have also played their role in removing community fears about contraception methods. This is the most unique and impressive approach adopted by FP programmes in Iran.[17] Social stigmas such as men's negative behaviours towards permanent contraception, were addressed through consultative sessions with non-state actor (ulema); however, political actors played a crucial role in these endeavours.[18,19]

In Egypt, the Grand Mufti, the country's most authoritative interpreter of Islamic law, issued a religious decree in the mid-1930 spermitting contraception, thus allowing the establishment of birth control clinics in Egyptian cities. He declared that the earliest followers of the Prophet (pbuh) practiced contraception with the knowledge of the Prophet, who did not forbid it. In 1964, Sheikh Hasan Ma'mun encouraged the use of contraception based on the changing needs of the Muslim people. Since 1980, religious leaders have played a major role in the public education efforts of the State Information Service by speaking out on the acceptability of birth control in the eyes of Islam.[20] In the 1990s, the National Population Commission made population issues part of the educational curriculum, including the religious educational curriculum.[21]

In Jordan, a lack of awareness and acceptance of contraceptives has been widely believed to be a socially constructed adherence to tradition, often with religious implications. Additionally, the doctrine of Islam has often been interpreted to forbid the use of FP methods. In fact, it is being argued that perhaps Muslim leaders' positions on FP are not always interpreted correctly; these leaders mayin fact, be no more opposed to reproductive health programmes than are other members of society.[22,23] Traditional, familial, and religious pressures on Jordanian women were limiting factors in birth spacing. Son preferences and religious norms among Jordanian women had a strong influence on contraceptive behaviours. The involvement of religious leaders in FP programmes had a positive influence on rural Jordanian women.[24] Family planning programmes supported through fatwas triggered the contraceptive uptake among Muslim communities. The government led FP programmes and the proactive role of religious leaders was effectively persuaded younger women to seek reproductive health services.[25]

In Kuwait, women held the perception that FP is not allowed in Islam. Today, contraception is generally accepted in Kuwait and is often considered more important for child spacing than for family size limitation. Although Kuwait did not have any state-funded FP programme, the government provided free contraceptive products and methods.[26]

[...]

Africa

In Morocco, the low use of contraceptives by women was attributed to hindrances by religious extremists. Research in Morocco established that religious extremists played a strong role in the misinterpretation of Islam about FP. However, the economic conditions of the working-class community could not be neglected while looking at the complex decision making process of reproductive health practices. Clergymen were therefore engaged in the national programme to help achieve desired results.[31]

In Nigeria, the majority of religious leaders emphasized the importance of sexuality education in schools, yet some disagreed. It was realized that religious leaders were aware of problems related to young people's reproductive health. However, today, it is felt that the harmonization of sexuality education in schools according to cultural values, is needed.[32]

Discussion

Religion remains a central issue in the discourse on FP and contraception despite the assiduous efforts of state programmes on FP and birth spacing and the proactive advocacy role played by non-government organizations (NGOs). The Quran does not disallow birth control, nor does it forbid a husband or wife from spacing pregnancies or limiting the number of children. Thus, the great majority of Islamic jurists believe that FP is permissible in Islam.[33] The silence of the Quran on the subject of contraception could not be a matter of omission by God, as he is "All-Knowing" and Islam is understood to be an eternal religion and a code of life. The proponents of FP also note that coitus interruptus or withdrawal was practiced in the epoch of the Prophet (pbuh) by his Companions.[34] The Quranic teaching for mothers to breastfeed their children for two years must be understood with its precise philosophy i.e. to allow women to have rest and restore their anatomical, physiological, and hormonal system before another pregnancy.[35] In its true spirit, Islam is considerate of FP as spacing pregnancies and curtailing the number of pregnancies makes

Family Planning in Malawi

For two villages in southern Malawi, climate change and contraception have become intertwined. So much so, that long-held cultural assumptions are starting to change.

Sheikh Mosa is chief of one of the villages, Mposa. He says there's been a massive shift in mindset toward family planning as people in the villages begin to feel the effects of population growth and climate change first-hand.

Look no further than the recent flooding in Malawi that has washed away many of his people's crops. Devastating floods in January displaced nearly a quarter million people, and half the country became an official disaster zone.

Mosa says the larger families in his village are struggling with hunger. With less food, kids drop out of school. Young girls may be forced into marriage or prostitution. But families with fewer children, he says, will find it easier to recover.

Mosa's village has been leading the family planning push in this part of Malawi. It formed a mother's support group that spreads the message of modern contraception and smaller family sizes through words and song. The group also rescues girls from child marriage and teenage pregnancy, ensuring they stay in school—all without a penny of outside financial support.

They're doing this not because someone is telling them to, or paying them to, but because, as Mosa says, their future depends on it.

According to the Guttmacher Institute, a reproductive health organization, more than four out of every ten women in Malawi lack access to modern contraception. Closing that gap has become a rallying cry for the southern Malawi villages of Ncheo and Mposa.

A local Chanco Community Radio program recently aired a discussion between the two villages. People talked about how the majority of women are opting for injectable forms of contraception, since they last longer. To get the injection, the women have to walk for up to a day to reach clinics. And demand is so high that the clinics say they don't have enough contraception to go around.

"God commanded' family planning, says this Muslim leader in flood-ravaged Malawi", by Sam Eaton, Public Radio International, March 12, 2015.

mothers more physically fit and fathers more financially at ease. None of these actions contravene any prohibition in the Quran or in the Prophet's (pbuh) tradition (Sunnah). If redundant fertility leads to a definite health nuisance for mothers and children, or economic hardship and discomfiture for fathers, or the helplessness of parents to raise their children properly, Muslims would be allowed to regulate their fertility in order to reduce these hardships.

The organized FP programmes of Egypt and Iran are noteworthy. Both often involve religious leaders in their FP campaigns. Egypt is home to Al-Azhar Mosque and Al-Azhar University, two renowned centres of Islamic teaching. These centres have frequently dispatched fatwas in favour of modern contraception and the Egyptian government has used them in its thriving FP campaigns.[36] As a consequence, contraceptives are available in Egypt in all government primary healthcare facilities. Since the reinstatement of Iran's national FP programme, the Ministry of Health and Medical Education in Tehran has regularly issued fatwas to its provincial offices and down to the lower strata of the health network to remove any doubts that health providers or clients may have about the permissibility of FP and contraception in Islam. Health clinics must display the fatwas for their clients as a ready reference. Moreover, the issuing of fatwas on FP is not the monopoly of the ministry of Health office in Tehran; these rulings can be sought from local clergies, as well.[37] However, there is a stern pre-requisite in this case—the capacity building of religious leaders. It is absolutely imperative that religious leaders and local clergymen possess accurate and appropriate information and skills to help their followers make informed choices on matters related to health and wellbeing, particularly on matters related to FP and birth spacing. There is a need to mobilize and sensitize these stakeholders to play their parts as a matter of social responsibility towards saving women from unwanted pregnancies and improving children's health.

For a country like Pakistan, the enormity of this emergency of population overgrowth coupled with illiteracy and poverty has emerged as a menace to the social system. It is a major impediment in the path of all efforts to improve living standards.[38] It is strongly suggested for all future interventions encompassing FP as their mainstay, to advocate the concept for the betterment of mother's and children's health. The concept of spacing children means the practice of contraception in order to allow a rational time period between the births of any two children: the point being that each child receives ample attention in its upbringing. A mother's full attention is required in the difficult task of nourishing, training, and educating a child. It is very difficult to provide this essential care and attention for each child if a baby is born every year. Moreover, according to Islamic jurisprudence, fatwas, and the case studies of various Islamic countries, it can be deduced that if another pregnancy would seriously affect the care and upbringing of an existing child, then reversible methods of birth control may be practiced. Family planning has always been tainted by its association with population control—the discredited attempts by various countries to reduce their populations through coercion. Hence, this approach has damaged the programme's overall spirit. Today, it is about global population planning where the number has crossed seven billion. Future interventions must provide FP, birth spacing, and general mother and child health services to women and girls around the world to eventually change the course of their lives. That is what will make the paradigm of FP transformational. In this regard, social marketing has shown successful results in bringing about behaviour change towards the uptake of birth spacing methods in Pakistan and elsewhere. However, since the coverage of social marketing was limited to urban and peri-urban areas of the country, the desired result of fertility control was not achieved, especially amongst rural women.

Conclusion

The issue of FP and contraception in Islam has become a grave concern because of unprecedented population growth around the globe; Indonesia and Pakistan are major contributors. Other

Islamic developing countries present maternal and child health indicators which are not on track to achieve the millennium development goals (MDGs) set for 2015. Having recognized that Islam is still the mainstay in the debate on FP and contraception in Islamic countries, religious leaders, ulema, scholars, think tanks, and even local clergymen should be disseminating the correct information and actively engaging in advocacy for the promotion of birth spacing for the improvement of maternal and child health outcomes. Improving literacy rates through investment in girls' education is another proven strategy to improve reproductive behaviours. This becomes even more relevant for the developing countries listed in this paper where maternal and child health indicators cannot be compared with those of the developed world.

References

1. Pakistan Demographic and Health Survey (PDHS) 2006-7. Islamabad, Pakistan: National Institute of Population Studies (NIPS); Macro International Ltd.; 2008.
2. International conference on population and development. Cairo: United Nations; 1994.
3. The millennium summit. New York (NY): United Nations; 2000.
4. Pasha O, Fikree FF, Vermund S. Determinants of unmet need for family planning in squatter settlements in Karachi, Pakistan. Asia Pac Popul J 2001;16(2):93-108.
5. Stephenson R, Hennink M. Barriers to family planning service use among the urban poor in Pakistan. Asia Pac Popul J 2004;19(2):5-26.
6. Ali M, Ushijima H. Perceptions of men on role of religious leaders in reproductive health issues in rural Pakistan. J Biosoc Sci 2005 Jan;37(1):115-22.
7. Douthwaite M, Ward P. Increasing contraceptive use in rural Pakistan: An evaluation of the lady health worker programme. Health Policy & Planning 2005;20(2):117-223.
8. Azmat SK. Mobilizing male opinion leaders' support for family planning to improve maternal health: A theory-based qualitative study from Pakistan. 2011; 4: 421-431. J Multidiscip Healthc 2011;4:421-31.
9. Nasir JA, inde A. Factors associated with contraceptive approval among religious leaders in Pakistan. 2011; 43: 587-596. J Biosoc Sci 2011;43:587-96.
10. Shaikh BT. Unmet need for family planning in Pakistan-PDHS 2006-7: It's time to re-examine déjà vu. Open Access Journal of Contraception 2010;1:113-8.
16. Vahidnia F. Case study: fertility decline in Iran. Population Environment 2007;28:259-66.
17. Rahnama P, Hidarnia A, Shokravi FA, Kazemnejad A, Ghazanfari Z, Montazeri A. Withdrawal users' experiences of and attitudes to contraceptive methods: A study from the eastern district of Tehran, Iran. BMC Public Health 2010;10(779).
18. Keramat A, Zarei A, rabi M. Barriers and facilitators affecting vasectomy acceptability (a multi stages study in a sample from north eastern Iran), 2005-2007. Asia Pacific Family Medicine 2011;10(1):5.
19. Simbar M. Achievements of the Iranian family planning programmes 1956-2006. East Mediterr Health J 2012;18(3):279-86.

20. Kats G . Family planning and the religious issue. 1983; 4(1):43-44. Cairo Today 1983;4(1):43-4.
21. Private practitioner family planning project. Family planning dialogue. Rumours of contraception: Myths vs. facts. New Egypt J Med 1990 1990;4(2):1-21.
22. Underwood C. Islamic precepts and family planning: The perceptions of Jordanian religious leaders and their constituents. International Family Planning Perspectives 2000;26(3):100-17.
23. Hasna F. Islam, Social traditions and family planning. 2003; 37(2): 181-197. Social Policy & Administration 2003;37(2):181-97.
24. Kridli SAO, Libbus K. . Contraception in Jordan: a cultural and religious perspective. Int Nurs Rev 2001;48(3):144-51.
25. Sueyoshi S, Ohtsuka R. Significant effects of fatwa-based perception on contraceptive practice among Muslim women in south Jordan under the early stage of fertility transition. Biodemography Soc Biol 2010;56(67):79.
26. Shah MA, Shah NM, Chowdhury RI, Menon I. Unmet need for contraception in Kuwait: issues for healthcare providers. Social Science & Medicine 2004;59(1573):1580.
31. Hughes CF. The "amazing" fertility decline: Islam, economics, and reproductive decision making among working-class Moroccan women. Med Anthropol Q 2011;25(4):417-35.
32. Ilika AL, Emelumadu OF, Okonkwo IP. Religious leaders' perceptions and support of reproductive health of young people in Anambra State, Nigeria. Niger Postgrad Med J 2006;13(2):111-6.
33. Atighetchi D. The position of Islamic tradition on contraception. Medicine & Law 1994;13(7-8):717-25.
34. Jütte R. Contraception - A history. Cambridge: Polity Press; 2008.
35. Hawwas AW. Breast feeding as seen by Islam. Population Science 1983;7:55-8.
36. Al-Azhar Islamic Research Academy Fatwa Committee. Al-Azhar fatwa committee's point of view on birth planning. Population Science 1988;8:15-7.
37. Roudi-Fahimi F. Iran's family planning program: responding to a nation's needs. Washington (DC): Population Reference Bureau; 2002.
38. Ministry of Finance. Economic Survey of Pakistan 2011-12. Islamabad, Pakistan: Government of Pakistan; 2012.

Conflict Between Religious Beliefs and Pediatric Care

Armand H. Matheny Antommaria, MD, PhD, FAAP
and Kathryn L. Weisem, MD, MA

In the following viewpoint, Armand H Matheny Antommaria and Kathryn L. Weise detail the conflicts among doctors providing appropriate pediatric care for children whose parents turn to unproven religious or spiritual healing practices, often to outcomes that put their children's lives at a serious disadvantage. Courts have argued that while parents have the right to refuse proven medical care, that right does not extend to the right of having their children potentially spread communicable diseases to other children, including ones who may be immuno-suppressed or are unable to be vaccinated for other health reasons. Antommaria is director of the Cincinnati Children's Ethics Center. Weise is a bioethics consultant staff physician and an associate professor of pediatrics at the Cleveland Clinic.

As you read, consider the following questions:

1. Should families have the right to refuse treatment for preventable illnesses because of religious exemption?
2. What are the connections between fundamentalist religious practices and childhood medical neglect?
3. What factors are evaluated in the review of cases of potential neglect?

"Conflicts Between Religious or Spiritual Beliefs and Pediatric Care: Informed Refusal, Exemptions, and Public Funding," by Armand H. Matheny Antommaria and Kathryn L. Weise, American Academy of Pediatrics, November 2013. Reprinted by permission.

R eligion plays an important role in the lives of many individuals. Fifty-eight percent of respondents to a recent poll reported that religion is very important in their lives, and 23% reported that it is fairly important.[1] The relationship between religion and medicine is complex. Some studies suggest "greater involvement in religion conveys more health-related benefits."[2] There are, however, times when religion and medicine conflict. The current policy statement addresses 3 related issues: (1) parents' refusal of medical treatment of their children; (2) religious exemptions to child abuse and neglect laws; and (3) public funding of alternative unproven religious or spiritual healing practices. The statement situates religious refusals within the scope of parental authority and argues that children's future autonomy should be protected. Religious exemption statutes do not protect all children equally and create uncertainty and, to protect children's health, should be repealed. Public health care funding should focus on established, effective therapies, and paying for spiritual healing practices may inadvertently engender medical neglect. The discussion of these specific topics should not be interpreted as a broader criticism of the interaction between religion and medicine.

Religious Objections to Medical Care

Although parents have broad authority, they have less discretion in making medical decisions for their children than for themselves. On the basis of the ethical principles of autonomy and respect for persons, capacitated adults should have wide license in making medical decisions for themselves, including the refusal of potentially life-saving medical treatment. Their liberty should only be limited in cases of direct harm to third parties, such as the risk of transmitting serious infectious diseases. Infants and children lack the ability to make autonomous medical decisions; therefore, the law generally authorizes their parents or guardians to make such decisions on their behalf. These decisions should primarily focus on the child's best interests.[3,4] Clinicians should afford parents and guardians significant discretion in their interpretation of these interests and collaborate with them to develop treatment plans that promote their children's health. Although family autonomy and privacy are important social values, parents' choices may be limited when they rise to the level of abuse or neglect.[5]

Failure to provide children with essential medical care has been increasingly recognized as a form of neglect. In 1983, the US Department of Health and Human Services (HHS) amended its definition of negligent treatment to include failure to provide adequate medical care.[6] A number of factors are relevant to the evaluation of suspected medical neglect, including likelihood and magnitude of the harm of foregoing medical treatment and the benefits, risks, and burdens of the proposed treatment.[7-9] For example, the risk of an individual unimmunized child contracting a communicable vaccine-preventable disease may be low if immunization rates in the community are high and disease prevalence is low.[10] Serious harms include death, severe disability, or severe pain. The American Academy of Pediatrics (AAP) Committee on Child Abuse and Neglect identifies a variety of factors that can lead to children not receiving appropriate medical care and corresponding graduated management options for pediatricians. For example, lack of awareness, knowledge, or skills can be addressed by counseling and education.[7] Ethics consultation is an additional management option.[7,11] If less-restrictive alternatives are not available or successful, pediatricians should refer families to child protective services agencies. In emergencies, providers may be ethically justified in administering treatment immediately necessary to preserve life, prevent serious disability, or treat severe pain. They should notify child protective services as soon as possible.

The basis for some parents' rejection of medical treatment is religious or spiritual. Traditions vary in the scope of medical treatments they refuse. For example, members of the Followers of Christ refuse all medical treatment in favor of prayer, anointing with oil, and the laying on of hands.[12] Christian Scientists may use dentists and physicians for "mechanical" procedures, such as setting bones or childbirth, but consider most illnesses to be the result of the individual's mental attitude and seek healing through spiritual means, such as prayer. They consider these healing practices incompatible with concurrent medical treatment.[13] Other religious groups prohibit only specific medical interventions. On the basis of their interpretation of scripture, Jehovah's Witnesses only prohibit the use of blood and its major fractions.[14] Understanding these differences is important in identifying whether there are mutually acceptable alternatives.

Some religious refusals have, tragically, led to children's deaths from readily treatable conditions, such as pneumonia, appendicitis, or diabetes.[12,15] Although the free exercise of religion, including parents teaching their children their religious beliefs, is an important societal value, it must be balanced against other important societal values, such as protecting children from serious harm.[16] In some situations, the issue is primarily an empirical one—the relative efficacy of medical and spiritual interventions. Although systematic empirical evidence of the efficacy of religious interventions is often lacking, the courts can judge efficacy by using criteria generally accepted by both parents and health care providers. In other situations, the issue involves differing conceptions of benefit and harm. Parents and guardians should have significant discretion in weighing the risks and benefits of a proposed treatment. At times, the primary benefit of refusing medical treatment or seeking alternative nonmedical treatment is religious or spiritual, such as the implications of the treatment on the patient's eternal salvation. In such cases, the potential benefit cannot be evaluated by using generally accepted criteria. In such situations, the child's future ability to decide this contested issue for himself or herself should be protected.[17] Some adolescents may possess adequate decision-making capacity to comprehend and evaluate the risks and benefits of medical treatment. The possibility of coercion should also be considered in the evaluation of whether a capacitated adolescent's dissent is autonomous.[18]

The courts have consistently ordered life-saving medical treatment over parental religious objections.[8,9] In passages frequently quoted in subsequent rulings, the US Supreme Court famously stated, "The right to practice religion freely does not include liberty to expose the community or the child to communicable disease or the latter to ill health or death" and "Parents may be free to become martyrs themselves. But it does not follow they are free, in identical circumstances, to make martyrs of their children before they have reached the age of full and legal discretion when they can make that choice for themselves."[19] There is less unanimity in judicial decisions if the condition is not life-threatening, the treatment has significant adverse effects, or the treatment has limited efficacy.[7-9] Courts may also consider the negative psychological effects of court-ordered treatment or medical foster care in their decisions.

Religious Exemptions to Child Abuse and Neglect Laws

Most states have "religious exemptions" to their child abuse and neglect laws. These exemptions proliferated in response to the Child Abuse Prevention and Treatment Act of 1974. The act stated, "Provided, however, that a parent or guardian legitimately practicing his religious beliefs who thereby does not provide specified medical treatment for a child, for that reason alone shall not be considered a negligent parent or guardian."[20] Enacting exemptions was a condition for states to receive federal child abuse grants. More than 40 states adopted exemptions, which vary in their location within each state's code and wording.[8] Some apply to child protective services agencies' ability to intervene, and others apply to parents' criminal liability. The HHS revised its position, taking a neutral stance, when the act was reauthorized in 1983: "Nothing in this part should be construed as requiring or prohibiting a finding of negligent treatment or maltreatment when a parent practicing his or her religious beliefs does not, for that reason alone, provide medical treatment for a child."[21] After reauthorization of the act in 1987, HHS clarified that reports of medical neglect should only be

Most States Allow Religious Exemptions from Child Abuse and Neglect Laws

All states have laws prohibiting child abuse and neglect. But in 34 states (as well as the District of Columbia, Guam and Puerto Rico), there are exemptions in the civil child abuse statutes when medical treatment for a child conflicts with the religious beliefs of parents, according to data collected by the U.S. Department of Health and Human Services.

These exemptions recently drew renewed attention in Idaho when, in May, a state task force released a report stating that five children there had died unnecessarily in 2013 because their parents, for religious reasons, had refused medical treatment for them. Such legal exemptions in Idaho and other states mean, for example, that if a parent withholds medical treatments for an ailing child and instead opts for spiritual treatment through prayer, the child will not to be considered "neglected" under the law, even if he or she dies. These exemptions are meant to accommodate the teachings of some religious groups, such as Christian Scientists and the Idaho-based Followers of Christ. Some of these groups urge and, in the case of Followers of Christ, sometimes mandate the use of faith-based healing practices in lieu of medical science.

Currently, 19 states and territories have no religious exemptions to civil child abuse and neglect statutes. In addition, Nevada and American Samoa have exemptions that do not specifically mention religion, but could apply to religion. For instance, American Samoa's statute says, "those investigating child abuse must take into account accepted child-rearing practices of the culture in which the child participates."

The exemptions came into being as a result of federal requirements that no longer exist; they grew out of the federal Child Abuse Prevention and Treatment Act (CAPTA), which was signed into law by President Richard Nixon in 1974. While that statute did not mention religious exemptions specifically, the requirements issued by what was then the Department of Health, Education and Welfare for states to receive federal funding specified that a religious exemption must be added to the state's child protection laws. The most recent reauthorization does not include a religious exemption.

"Most states allow religious exemptions from child abuse and neglect laws", by Aleksandra Sandstrom, Pew Research Center, August 12, 2016. Reprinted by Permission.

made if there is harm or a substantial risk of harm, and religious exemptions should be a matter of state discretion rather than federal imposition.[18] A number of states subsequently amended or repealed their religious exemption statutes.[8,16] Most recently, after the deaths of 2 children, Oregon repealed its exemption.[22]

The AAP believes that religious exemptions to state child abuse and neglect laws should be repealed. These exemptions fail to provide an equivalent level of protection to children whose parents practice spiritual healing and children whose parents do not.[16] In addition, they may create confusion that results in harm to children; parents may be unclear about their duty to provide medical treatment, child protective services agencies may falsely believe that they cannot intervene until after a child suffers serious injury or dies, and prosecutors and courts may be uncertain whether parents are subject to criminal liability if their child dies of medical neglect.[5,16] Although the exemptions could be revised to make it explicit that seeking medical care is required when a child is seriously ill,[5,8] repeal is preferable because it provides greater clarity.[16] For example, parents and spiritual healers who are members of groups that refuse all medical treatment may not be able to differentiate moderate from severe illnesses and, therefore, fail to seek medical attention in a timely manner.[14,16]

Public Funding of Spiritual Healing Practices

In addition to efforts to create religious exemptions, some churches and legislators have sought to provide public funds to pay for religious or spiritual healing practices. For example, Medicare and Medicaid cover care provided at Christian Science sanatoria and other religious nonmedical health care institutions and exempt these institutions from medical oversight requirements.[23] In addition, there were unsuccessful efforts to include coverage of Christian Science practitioners in the 2009 federal health care reform bills[24] and ongoing efforts to include their services in the essential health benefits package. These efforts should be distinguished from both health care services provided by religious organizations, such as Roman Catholic and Seventh-day Adventist hospitals, and pastoral care provided as a bundled service.

Coverage for unproven care by unlicensed practitioners is poor public policy for several reasons. Fundamentally, public funds should be spent on established, effective therapies.[25] In addition, religious nonmedical health care institutions provide custodial rather than skilled nursing care, a benefit not covered in other institutions. Given patients' exemptions from undergoing medical examinations, it is not possible to determine whether patients of religious nonmedical health care institutions would otherwise qualify for benefits.[23,26] Because providing public funding for unproven alternative spiritual healing practices may be perceived as legitimating these services, parents may not believe that they have an obligation to seek medical treatment. Although the AAP recognizes the importance of addressing children's spiritual needs as part of the comprehensive care of children, it opposes public funding of religious or spiritual healing practices.

References

1. Gallup. Religion. Available at: www.gallup.com/poll/1690/religion.aspx. Accessed April 21, 2013
2. Krause N. Religion and health: making sense of a disheveled literature. J Relig Health. 2011;50(1):20–35pmid:20614186
3. American Academy of Pediatrics, Committee on Bioethics. Informed consent, parental permission, and assent in pediatric practice. Pediatrics. 1995;95(2):314–317pmid:7838658
4. Ross LF. Children, Families, and Health Care Decision Making. Oxford, UK: Clarendon Press; 1998
5. Gathings JT Jr. When rights clash: the conflict between a parent's right to free exercise of religion versus his child's right to life. Cumberland Law Rev. 1988–1989;19(3):585–616
6. Child Abuse and Neglect Prevention and Treatment, 45 CFR § 1340.2(d)(2)(i) (1983)
7. Jenny C, Committee on Child Abuse and Neglect, American Academy of Pediatrics. Recognizing and responding to medical neglect. Pediatrics. 2007;120(6):1385–1389pmid:18055690
8. Malecha WF. Faith healing exemptions to child protection laws: keeping the faith versus medical care for children. J Legis. 1985;12(2):243–263
9. Trahan J. Constitutional law: parental denial of a child's medical treatment for religious reasons. Annu Surv Am Law. 1989;1989(1):307–341pmid:16594107
10. Diekema DS, American Academy of Pediatrics Committee on Bioethics. Responding to parental refusals of immunization of children. Pediatrics. 2005;115(5):1428–1431pmid:15867060

11. American Academy of Pediatrics. Committee on Bioethics. Institutional ethics committees. Pediatrics. 2001;107(1):205–209pmid:11134464

12. Mayes S. Another Followers of Christ couple indicted in death of a child. The Oregonian. July 31, 2010. Available at: www.oregonlive.com/oregon-city/index.ssf/2010/07/another_followers_of_christ_couple_indicted_in_death_of_a_child.html. Accessed August 15, 2012

13. Talbot NA. The position of the Christian Science church. N Engl J Med. 1983;309(26):1641–1644pmid:6646189

14. Dixon JL, Smalley MG. Jehovah's Witnesses. The surgical/ethical challenge. JAMA. 1981;246(21):2471–2472pmid:7299971

15. Asser SM, Swan R. Child fatalities from religion-motivated medical neglect. Pediatrics. 1998;101(4 pt 1):625–629pmid:9521945

16. Monopoli PA. Allocating the costs of parental free exercise: striking a new balance between sincere religious belief and a child's right to medical treatment. Pepperdine Law Rev. 1991;18(2):319–352pmid:11652074

17. Sheldon M. Ethical issues in the forced transfusion of Jehovah's Witness children. J Emerg Med. 1996;14(2):251–257pmid:8740763

18. Guichon J, Mitchell I. Medical emergencies in children of orthodox Jehovah's Witness families: three recent legal cases, ethical issues and proposals for management. Paediatr Child Health (Oxford). 2006;11(10):655–658pmid:19030248

19. Prince v Massachusetts, 321 US 158, 170 (1944)

20. Child Abuse and Neglect Prevention and Treatment Act, 45 CFR § 1340.1-2(b) (1975)

21. Child Abuse and Neglect Prevention and Treatment Act, 45 CFR § 1340.2(d)(2)(ii) (1983)

22. Mayes S. Kitzhaber signs bill to eliminate religious defense for faith-healing parents. The Oregonian. June 16, 2011. Available at: www.oregonlive.com/oregon-city/index.ssf/2011/06/kitzhaber_signs_bill_to_eliminate_religious_defense_for_faith-healing_parents.html. Accessed August 15, 2012

23. Harris BR. Veiled in textual neutrality: is that enough? A candid reexamination of the constitutionality of Section 4454 of the Balanced Budget Act of 1997. Alabama Law Rev. 2010;61(2):393–423

24. Wan W. 'Spiritual health care' raises church-state concerns. The Washington Post. November 23, 2009. Available at: www.washingtonpost.com/wp-dyn/content/article/2009/11/22/AR2009112202216.html. Accessed August 15, 2012

25. Libby R, Committee on Child Health Financing American Academy of Pediatrics. Principles of health care financing. Pediatrics. 2010;126(5):1018–1021pmid:20974786

26. Children's Health Care Is a Legal Duty Inc v Min de Parle, 212 F.3d 1084 (8th Cir. 2000), cert. denied, 532 US 957 (2001)]

In the United States Parents Refuse Medical Care for Children in the Name of Christ

Jason Wilson

In the following viewpoint Jason Wilson tells the story of faith-based protections in Idaho, which allow fundamentalist religious sects like the Followers of Christ to refuse necessary medical care in the name of their religion. These sects have led to the deaths of countless children in Idaho, which takes advantage of a provision in the 1974 Child Abuse Prevention and Treatment Act (CAPTA), signed by President Richard Nixon. Two architects of the act, J. R. Haldeman and John Ehrlichman, were Christian Scientists who did not believe that the government should force religious organizations to participate in medical care. The provision the two crafted stated that those who believe prayer is the only way to cure illness are exempted from the law. Wilson is a writer whose works have appeared in the Guardian *and other publications.*

"Letting them die: parents refuse medical help for children in the name of Christ," by Jason Wilson, *Guardian* News and Media Limited, April 13, 2016. Reprinted by Permission.

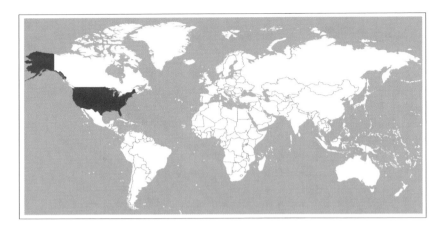

As you read, consider the following questions:

1. Should states like Idaho protect families who use their religious beliefs to excuse medical neglect?
2. What are the differences between the laws protecting children in Oregon and Idaho?
3. How do states like Idaho benefit from allowing organizations like the Followers of Christ to continue to allow children to die by calling it "God's will"?

M ariah Walton's voice is quiet—her lungs have been wrecked by her illness, and her respirator doesn't help. But her tone is resolute.

"Yes, I would like to see my parents prosecuted."

Why?

"They deserve it." She pauses. "And it might stop others."

Mariah is 20 but she's frail and permanently disabled. She has pulmonary hypertension and when she's not bedridden, she has to carry an oxygen tank that allows her to breathe. At times, she has had screws in her bones to anchor her breathing device. She may soon have no option for a cure except a heart and lung transplant—an extremely risky procedure.

All this could have been prevented in her infancy by closing a small congenital hole in her heart. It could even have been successfully treated in later years, before irreversible damage was done. But Mariah's parents were fundamentalist Mormons who went off the grid in northern Idaho in the 1990s and refused to take their children to doctors, believing that illnesses could be healed through faith and the power of prayer.

As she grew sicker and sicker, Mariah's parents would pray over her and use alternative medicine. Until she finally left home two years ago, she did not have a social security number or a birth certificate.

Had they been in neighboring Oregon, her parents could have been booked for medical neglect. In Mariah's case, as in scores of others of instances of preventible death among children in Idaho since the 1970s, laws exempt dogmatic faith healers from prosecution, and she and her sister recently took part in a panel discussion with lawmakers at the state capitol about the issue. Idaho is one of only six states that offer a faith-based shield for felony crimes such as manslaughter.

Some of those enjoying legal protection are fringe Mormon families like Mariah's, many of whom live in the state's north. But a large number of children have died in southern Idaho, near Boise, in families belonging to a reclusive, Pentecostal faith-healing sect called the Followers of Christ.

In Canyon County, just west of the capital, the sect's Peaceful Valley cemetery is full of graves marking the deaths of children who lived a day, a week, a month. Last year, a taskforce set up by Idaho governor Butch Otter estimated that the child mortality rate for the Followers of Christ between 2002 and 2011 was 10 times that of Idaho as a whole.

The shield laws that prevent prosecutions in Idaho are an artifact of the Nixon administration. High-profile child abuse cases in the 1960s led pediatricians and activists to push for laws that combatted it. In order to help states fund such programs,

Congress passed the Child Abuse Prevention and Treatment Act (Capta), which Richard Nixon signed in 1974.

But there was a fateful catch due to the influence of Nixon advisers John Ehrlichman and J. R. Haldeman, both lifelong Christian Scientists.

Boston College history professor Alan Rogers explains how the men—later jailed for their role in the Watergate scandal – were themselves members of a faith-healing sect, and acted to prevent their co-religionists being charged with crimes of neglect.

"Because Ehrlichman and Haldeman were Christian Scientists, they had inserted into the law a provision that said those who believe that prayer is the only way to cure illness are exempted from this law," he said.

They also ensure that states had to pass similar exemptions in order to access Capta funds. The federal requirement was later relaxed, but the resultant state laws have had to be painstakingly repealed one by one.

Some states, such as Oregon, held on longer until high-profile deaths in the Followers of Christ church in Oregon City attracted the attention of local media; over time the state reversed course.

As a result, several Followers of Christ members in Oregon have been successfully prosecuted. In 2010, Jeffrey and Marci Beagley were convicted of criminally negligent homicide after the death of their toddler, Neal, who died from a congenital bladder blockage. In 2011, Timothy and Rebecca Wyland were convicted of criminal mistreatment and the court ordered that their daughter Aylana be medically treated for the growth that had been threatening to blind her. Later that year, Dale and Shannon Hickman were convicted of second-degree manslaughter two years after their newborn son died of a simple infection.

Next door, Idaho presents a polar opposition to Oregon. Republicans, who enjoy an effective permanent majority in the state house, are surprisingly reluctant to even consider reform. Last year, the governor's Task Force on Children at Risk recommended change: "Religious freedoms must be protected; but vulnerable children must also be appropriately protected from unnecessary harm and death." Democratic legislator John Gannon proposed a repeal bill which he "never thought would really be that controversial."

The chairman of the senate health and welfare committee, Lee Heider, refused to even grant it a hearing, effectively killing it.

Hoyt is a fit 43, and lives in a well-scrubbed suburban neighborhood. He runs a successful window cleaning business that started with a squeegee mop and a bucket after his teenage escape from home left him with no cash and few educational opportunities. When I visited him, his house was being renovated —what was once a "barebones bachelor pad" now accommodates his partner and step-children. Slowly, Hoyt has developed the capacity for family life, after a life in the sect left him "unable to relate to families" for a long time. "I didn't understand the concept," he said.

He lost his faith around the age of five, when a baby died in his arms in the course of a failed healing. While elders prayed, Hoyt was in charge of removing its mucus with a suction device. He was told that the child died because of his own lack of faith. Something snapped, and he remembers thinking: "How can this possibly be God's work?" His apostasy set up lifelong conflicts with his parents and church elders.

In just one incident, when he was 12, Hoyt broke his ankle during a wrestling tryout. "I ended up shattering two bones in my foot," he said. His parents approached the situation with the usual Followers remedies—rubbing the injury with "rancid olive oil" and having him swig on Kosher wine.

Intermittently, they would have him attempt to walk. Each time, "my body would just go into shock and I would pass out."

"I would wake up to my step-dad, my uncles and the other elders of the church kicking me and beating me, calling me a fag, because I didn't have enough faith to let God come in and heal me, while my mom and my aunts were sitting there watching. And that's called faith healing."

He had so much time off with the untreated fracture that his school demanded a medical certificate to cover the absence. Forced to take him to a doctor, his mother spent most of the consultation accusing the doctor of being a pedophile.

He was given a cast and medication but immediately upon returning home, the medication was flushed down the toilet, leaving him with no pain relief. His second walking cast was cut off by male relatives at home with a circular saw.

Other people who have left the group, such as Linda Martin, told similar tales of coercion, failed healing using only rancid olive oil, and a high level of infant mortality, isolation and secrecy. Violence, she said, was "the reason I left home. My childhood and Brian's were very similar." Deaths from untreated illness are attributed to "God's will. Their lives are dominated by God's will."

Martin and Hoyt have both lobbied to change the laws, with Martin in particular devoting years of patient research to documenting deaths and other church activities. Hoyt has faced harassment online and at his home, and church members have even tried to undermine his business.

So far, their testimonies of abuse have not convinced Idaho's Republican legislators. Senator Heider, for one, describes the Followers of Christ as "very nice people".

Child advocate and author Janet Hei.mich, who has campaigned against exemptions around the country, says that Heider told her before the legislative session began that "he would carry the bill" and helped with the production of a draft, but by the time the session began in October he indicated that no bill would be passed or even heard.

Heider's repeated response to these claims was a welter of contradictions and bluster.

After telling the Guardian that no bill was lodged (John Gannon confirmed that he did, as was reported in local media in

February) and that he had been told by the attorney general and the Canyon County prosecuting attorney that the laws did not need to change (both men deny saying this), Heider took refuge in the US constitution.

"Republicans didn't feel the need to change the laws. We believe in the first amendment to the constitution. I don't think that states have a right to interfere in religions."

When pressed on the fact that children are dying unnecessarily as a result of exemptions, Heider makes an odd comparison.

"Are we going to stop Methodists from reading the New Testament? Are we going to stop Catholics receiving the sacraments? That's what these people believe in. They spoke to me and pointed to a tremendous number of examples where Christ healed people in the New Testament."

Heider blamed outsiders for stirring the pot on this issue, even challenging the Guardian's right to take an interest in the story, asking "what difference does it make to you?" and adding "is the United States coming in and trying to change Idaho's laws?" He confirmed that he attended a Followers of Christ service last year —a rare privilege for an outsider from a group that refuses to speak to reporters.

But if we take Heider at his word concerning the reasons for his opposition, his view of the constitution is simply mistaken.

Alan Rogers, the Boston College history professor, points to a string of US supreme court decisions that distinguish between freedom of belief and freedom of practice, which affirm the former and limit the latter where it causes harm. These stretch back as far as *Reynolds v United States* in 1878, which forbade Mormon polygamy, and include *Prince v Massachusetts*, which affirmed the federal government's ability to secure the welfare of children even when it conflicts with religious belief.

Frederick Clarkson, a senior fellow at Political Research Associates, has long researched the connection between religion and conservatism. He points out that "almost all American politicians are cowards when it comes to religion."

Religious liberty is a powerful idea, and a great achievement in the history of western civilization, but "it's also used as a tool by the rich and the powerful, and by politicians who want to look the other way."

There's also the fact that conservatives have been mobilizing religious liberty in recent years, first as a reason to kill same-sex marriage at the state level, and now to limit the scope of the supreme court's decision that it cannot be outlawed by states.

While Idaho legislators stonewall, children in faith-healing communities continue to suffer.

According to coroners' reports, in Canyon County alone just in the past decade at least 10 children in the Followers of Christ church have died. These include 15-year-old Arrian Granden, who died in 2012 after contracting food poisoning. She vomited so much that her esophagus ruptured. Untreated, she bled to death.

The other deaths are mostly infants who died during at-home births or soon after from treatable complications, simple infections or pneumonia.

In one Canyon County report on the death of an infant called Asher Sevy, we see the difficulty that the shield laws create for local authorities.

When Sevy died in 2006, a Canyon County coroner's deputy attended by two sherriff's deputies asked to take the body away for an autopsy. According to the coroner's account, the family "were very much against this for any reason", and informed the deputy that she "was not going with me or anyone else" and removal would have to be done "forcefully."

After a liaison with the county's chief deputy and the prosecutor's office, the assembled county officials decided to leave "rather than escalate a problem that could be worse than it was now." The conclusion? "The cause [of death] will go down as undetermined."

Autopsies are at the coroner's discretion, and the deputy, Bill Kirby, did write that at the time there was "no evidence of a crime." The incident is unsettling, though.

Canyon County coroner Vicki DeGeus-Morriss, who has been in office since 1991, refused to speak directly with the Guardian. However Joe Decker, a county spokesman, insisted that the coroner and other officials had been successful in building a better relationship with the Followers.

"Back when Vicki first took office, the Followers rarely, if ever, reported a death. And when they did, they would often be uncooperative with both the Coroner and law enforcement when they arrived on scene," Decker said. Now, they "have a relationship in which every single death is reported and autopsies are almost always performed."

For the outsider, there may still be something unsatisfying about this—a lingering impression that exemptions from child abuse prosecutions have led Followers to form the impression that the law can be negotiated with.

Nevertheless, local officials can't make laws, only enforce them. The frustration at the local effects of shield laws was perhaps evident in the support that Canyon County prosecutor Brian Taylor gave to efforts to change the laws.

Campaigners such as Mariah Walton, Janet Heimlich, Linda Martin and Brian Hoyt are determined not to let this matter rest in the next legislative session.

A new "Let Them Live" campaign, involving a television ad campaign featuring Mariah, is being coordinated by Bruce Wingate at Protect Idaho Kids. Resources are limited, but all are confident that improved public awareness will build pressure on legislators.

Gannon, the Democratic legislator, says for his part that his bill will be back next year. "It's not going to go away," he says. "Dead children don't care about the first amendment."

Periodical and Internet Sources Bibliography

The following articles have been selected to supplement the diverse views presented in this chapter.

Robert Barnes, "Supreme Court says crisis pregnancy centers do not have to provide women abortion information," *Washington Post*, June 26, 2018. https://www.washingtonpost.com/politics/ courts_law/supreme-court-says-crisis-pregnancy-centers-do-not- have-to-tell-women-about-abortion-information/2018/06/26/ d2b9f5c2-7943-11e8-80be-6d32e182a3bc_story. html?noredirect=on&utm_term=.17e65f7d6dcd.

Laura Bassett, "What Are 'Crisis Pregnancy Centers,' And Why Does The Supreme Court Care About Them?" Huffington Post, November 13, 2017. https://www.huffingtonpost. com/entry/crisis-pregancy-centers-supreme-court_ us_5a09f40ae4b0bc648a0d13a2.

Rothna Begum, "The Middle East's Women Are Championing Their Own Change," Human Rights Watch, March 7, 2018. https:// www.hrw.org/news/2018/03/07/middle-easts-women-are- championing-their-own-change.

Benjamin G. Bishin and Feryal M. Cherif, "The big gains for women's rights in the Middle East, explained," *Washington Post*, July 23, 2018. https://www.washingtonpost.com/news/monkey-cage/ wp/2018/07/23/womens-rights-are-advancing-in-the-middle- east-this-explains-why/?utm_term=.b6c8df80b15c.

Carla Bleiker, "Women's rights in the Islamic world," DW.com, September 27, 2017. https://www.dw.com/en/womens-rights-in- the-islamic-world/a-40714427.

Heather D Boonstra, "Islam, Women and Family Planning: A Primer," December 1, 2001. https://www.guttmacher.org/gpr/2001/12/ islam-women-and-family-planning-primer.

Amy G. Bryant and Jonas J. Swartz, "Why Crisis Pregnancy Centers Are Legal but Unethical", *AMA Journal of Ethics*, March

2018. https://journalofethics.ama-assn.org/article/why-crisis-pregnancy-centers-are-legal-unethical/2018-03.

Aimee Green, "Are decades of needless child deaths a thing of the past for the Followers of Christ?" *Oregonian*, July 15, 2018. https://www.oregonlive.com/expo/news/erry-2018/07/c6430fe46a2145/are-decades-of-needless-child.html.

Ali Mohammad Mir and Gul Rashida Shaikh, "Islam and family planning: changing perceptions of health care providers and medical faculty in Pakistan," *GHSP Journal*, August 1, 2013. http://www.ghspjournal.org/content/1/2/228.

Paul Offit, "Doctor to Legislators: Refusing Medical Care Isn't Religious Freedom," NBC News, March 9, 2015. https://www.nbcnews.com/health/kids-health/doctor-legislators-refusing-medical-care-isn-t-religious-freedom-n320031.

Robert Orr, "Faith-Based Decisions: Parents Who Refuse Appropriate Care for Their Children, Commentary 1," *AMA Journal of Ethics*, August 2003. https://journalofethics.ama-assn.org/article/faith-based-decisions-parents-who-refuse-appropriate-care-their-children-commentary-1/2003-08.

Genevra Pittman, "Don't let religious beliefs impede kids' care: doctors," Reuters, October 27, 2013. https://www.reuters.com/article/us-religion-kids/dont-let-religious-beliefs-impede-kids-care-doctors-idUSBRE99R03J20131028.

Carissa Wolf, "Medical care could have saved his brother's life. His parents prayed instead." *Idaho Statesman*, February 20, 2018. https://www.idahostatesman.com/news/politics-government/state-politics/article201203274.html.

CHAPTER 4

The Importance of Having Access to Reproductive Care Around the World

Countries Around the World Beat the US on Paid Parental Leave

Jessica Deahl

In the following viewpoint, Jessica Deahl shows that of the 193 countries that participate in the United Nations, the United States is one of a small handful of countries that do not have parental leave laws in place. The other countries include New Guinea, Suriname, and a few South Pacific island nations, which makes the United States one of the largest and most powerful countries in the world that does not have federal protections for parents. Countries like France and Canada have social insurance structures where small contributions create a pool of money that workers can draw from when they need to take leave, something the United States lacks. Deahl is editor for NPR's All Things Considered.

As you read, consider the following questions:

1. Why is the United States one of the only major developed countries to not offer paid parental leave? How does this impact families and especially women in the workplace?
2. What is the UN minimum for parental leave? Is it enough time? Why or why not?
3. What are the benefits of having paid parental leave for both parents, not just the mother?

Out of 193 countries in the United Nations, only a small handful do not have a national paid parental leave law: New Guinea, Suriname, a few South Pacific island nations and the United States.

In the U.S., that means a lot moms and dads go back to work much sooner after the birth of a baby than they would like because they can't afford unpaid time off.

Jody Heymann, founding director of the World Policy Analysis Center at UCLA, says the global landscape for paid parental leave looks bright, but the U.S. is far behind.

"The U.S. is absolutely the only high-income country that doesn't, and as you can tell by the numbers, overwhelmingly the world provides it," she says. "The world not only provides paid maternity leave, but they provide adequate paid paternity leave."

Countries first began thinking about paid parental leave during the Industrial Revolution, Heymann says.

"In the 1800s—as soon as women started moving from working at home to working in factories—countries realized they needed to do something to ensure that women could work and care," she says. "So they started to provide across Europe and across Latin America and elsewhere paid maternity leave—leave that would care for families, for kids and ensure that economies could succeed."

Later on, representatives from around the world met through the United Nations and agreed to strive for a minimum of 14 weeks of leave, paid at two-thirds of a worker's salary up to a cap. This was decades ago, and today, most countries meet or exceed that minimum. Heymann says at least 50 countries now provide six months or more of paid maternity leave.

The driving motivation behind setting a global standard for paid parental leave comes down to common sense and economic benefits, Heymann says.

"In most countries, families rely on income from both the mom and dad," she says. "Families can't afford to have a lengthy period without income for one of them. At the same time, newborns absolutely need parental care. So this being a fundamental piece of social insurance or what governments do as part of their social security really is common sense.

"The second piece that drives countries is I've spoken to finance ministers from around the world who say one of their greatest sources of success economically is getting women into the workforce in equal numbers," Heymann continues.

Brigitte Beltre, a mother from France, explains a common way that countries pay for this leave.

"You have to know it's not for free," she says. "In France, you have to work a certain amount of time to have paid maternity leave. You have to give to the system. It's like a savings account."

Governments rely on a social insurance structure, where small contributions create a pool of money that workers can draw from when they need to take leave.

"Those contributions to the government may come from employers, employees and the government's general revenue, but they pay it through a social insurance system, so that no business has a heavy burden—if they're a small employer and one person's out, or if they're a larger employer, but disproportionately have young parents as employees," Heymann says. "That's how they spread the responsibility evenly."

Canada has a similar set-up to France. Tatiana Mellema in Vancouver says being able to dip into that fund gave her enough time off to bounce back from the major medical event of giving birth.

"Physically the recovery of having a child is huge," Mellema says. "It took, for me, months."

She says it also gave her time to care for her new son at his most vulnerable stage.

"The financial support was essential to getting us through that year and giving me that time with him," Mellema says. "Had I not have had it, I probably would have had to go back to work fairly quickly after I had him, which I can't even imagine doing, because my experience is just having that year with him was so important."

Heymann says paid parental leave policies have a significant impact on infant and maternal health.

"So there are powerful, long-term studies showing that providing paid maternity leave, for example, lowers infant mortality," she says. "Beyond this, we know that women who have sufficient paid maternity leave are much more likely to breastfeed, and breastfeeding lowers the risk of all sorts of infectious diseases, it increases and improves cognitive outcomes, and it benefits the woman's health."

In Sweden, the government provides almost 16 months of paid leave to be used between two parents.

Per Einarsson, a video game developer who lives in Stockholm, Sweden, says he and his partner, Kristina, split that paid time off evenly when each of their two kids were born. He says that time helped him to be a more engaged dad.

"It was nice to be educated, if you may, to learn how to take care of my children and to bond with them, and then of course it was nice to give Kristina the possibility to get back to her job and focus on her career as well," he says.

Einarsson says that time set a tone in their home — one that's felt years later. Their kids are now three and five years old.

"I think in their eyes we were always very equal to them and still are," he says. "And I think that felt good to us and hopefully to our children as well."

But Sweden is not the norm. Most countries don't offer equal leave to men and women. Policies around the world tend to be more centered on moms than dads. But Heymann says the most competitive countries that do provide it show that paid paternity leave is economically possible.

"Overwhelmingly, the most competitive countries in the world—the ones with the strongest economies and the lowest unemployment—do provide paid leave for dads, showing this is feasible," she says.

And when women do get or take more paid leave than men, there can be an unintended downside: It makes it harder for women of child-bearing age to get hired or promoted.

In China, many mothers experience workplace discrimination after taking maternity leave despite laws that prohibit it.

"Although the labor law forbids the employer to fire female employees in one year after giving birth, the bosses can find ways to let the employee feel uncomfortable," says Meng Meng, a mother who lives in China.

Lama Dossary of Saudia Arabia says taking paid leave changed how she was treated at work. There, mothers receive 10 weeks of paid time off, and fathers get three days.

"When I went back I did feel like it did affect how I was looked at, how I was treated," Dossary says. "My promotions got stopped for a while. I wasn't given the same amount of work, I wasn't given the same amount of responsibility.

"I don't know how it would affect things, but I do think that maybe if other people were able to take such leave off — whether to take care of their older parents or a father maybe has to take some time off because he has a child that needs special care for a while—I think that would at least change the perception," she says.

According to Heymann, the U.S. is an outlier in a few ways when it comes to global parental leave polices.

On one hand, the U.S. is the only developed country without a national paid parental leave policy.

"We urgently need to catch up in the United States," Heymann says. "For a high-income country, we have some of the worst outcomes for our infants. We have some of the highest rates of infant mortality. We have huge health inequalities."

But despite this, Heymann says the U.S. stands out in one pretty positive way.

The U.S. Family and Medical Leave Act guarantees 12 weeks of job-protected time off equally to many American moms and dads. People caring for a sick parent or even themselves during a long illness also qualify.

Heymann points to this law as a good starting point because it treats mothers and fathers equally. But this is unpaid leave, and it doesn't apply to about half of the American work force.

"The problem is the fact that it's unpaid means it's unaffordable to many Americans," Heymann says. "And all of the caveats that come with the Family [and] Medical Leave Act that have to do with how many hours you've worked, how big your employer is, etc., means that millions of Americans aren't covered. So we need to take that basis, make it paid and ensure that all Americans are covered."

In East Africa and Southern Africa HIV and AIDS Hit Hardest

Avert.org

In the following excerpted viewpoint, writers at AVERT.org detail the impact of HIV and AIDS-related diseases on East and Southern Africa. The area is home to only 6.2 percent of the world's population, but over half the total number of people living with HIV—19.4 million. In 2016, Lesotho reported HIV in 25 percent of its population, the second-highest in the world, but among sex workers, the prevalence is 72 percent, and 38 percent in men who have sex with men. While condom use can help stop the transmission of HIV, many people in these countries either do not have access to them or do not know how they can help. Fortunately, the overall rate of infection is falling in the region, especially the rates in children up to age fourteen. AVERT is an organization that promotes education and understanding of HIV and AIDS.

As you read, consider the following questions:

1. Why are there such high rates of HIV infections in East and Southern Africa?
2. How many people died of AIDS-related illnesses in the region in 2016? What were some of the contributing factors?
3. What are the prevention programs in place in East and Southern Africa? Which are the most effective?

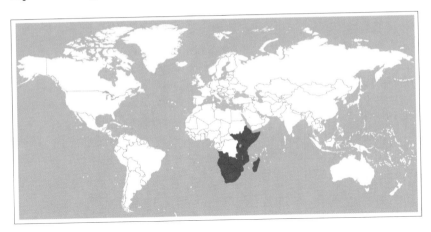

E ast and Southern Africa is the region hardest hit by HIV. It is home to 6.2% of the world's population but over half of the total number of people living with HIV in the world (19.4 million people). In 2016, there were 790,000 new HIV infections, 43% of the global total.[1]

South Africa accounted for one third (270,000) of the region's new infections in 2016. Another 50% occurred in eight countries: Mozambique, Kenya, Zambia, Tanzania, Uganda, Zimbabwe, Malawi, and Ethiopia.[2]

Just under half a million people (420,000) died of AIDS-related illnesses in the region in 2016, although the number of deaths has fallen significantly from 760,000 in 2010.[3]

Despite the continuing severity of the epidemic, huge strides have been made towards meeting the UNAIDS 90-90-90 targets. In 2016, 76% of people living with HIV were aware of their status, 79% of them were on treatment (equivalent to 60% of all people living with HIV in the region), and 83% of those on treatment had achieved viral suppression (equivalent to half of all people living with HIV in the region).[4]

Between 2010 and 2016, new HIV infections declined by 56% among children (0–14 years) to 77,000. New infections among adults declined by 29% over the same period, although there is significant variation between countries. Declines were greatest in Mozambique, Uganda and Zimbabwe. While in Ethiopia and Madagascar, the annual number of new infections increased.[5]

Women account for 56% of adults living with HIV in the region.[6] Young women (aged 15–24 years) accounted for 26% of new HIV infections in 2016, despite making up just 10% of the population.[7]

Although East and Southern Africa's HIV epidemic is driven by sexual transmission and is generalised, meaning it affects the population as a whole, certain groups such as sex workers and men who have sex with men have significantly higher HIV prevalence rates. For example, in 2016 Lesotho reported HIV prevalence among the general population at 25%, the second highest in the world, yet prevalence was even higher among sex workers at 72% and men who have sex with men at 33%.[8]

Groups most affected by HIV in East and Southern Africa

Young women and HIV in East and Southern Africa

In 2016, HIV prevalence among young women (15–24 years) in the region was double that of young men (3.4% compared to 1.6%), and in some countries the disparity between genders is even greater.[9]

The reasons behind this are numerous and complex. For example, the existence of high levels of transactional sex and age-disparate sexual relationships in many countries increase young women's HIV vulnerability.[10] Studies from Zimbabwe and Uganda, which have marriage patterns comparable with many other parts of the region, found young married women with partners who were 16 or more years older than them were at three times greater risk of HIV infection than those with partners 0–15 years older than themselves.[11]

A 2014 UNAIDS assessment of demographic and health surveys carried out in the region suggests young women face higher levels of spousal physical or sexual violence than women from other age groups.[12] Again, this heightens HIV risk—for example, a South African study found young women who experienced intimate partner violence were 50% more likely to have HIV than young women who had not experienced violence.[13]

Although knowledge among young people is improving, only 37% of young women and 41% of young men have comprehensive and correct knowledge of HIV prevention.[14] In addition, only 29% of adolescent women (aged 15–19) at high risk of HIV infection used a condom the last time they had sex, compared to 44% of their male counterparts.[15] Such low levels of condom use may be partly reflective of the fact that around half of the region's countries impose age-restrictions on buying condoms.[16]

[…]

Sex workers and HIV in East and Southern Africa

Although sex workers are disproportionately affected by HIV in every country in the region, HIV prevalence among this population varies greatly between countries, ranging from 1.3% in Madagascar to more than 70% in Lesotho and Namibia. In Botswana, Malawi, Rwanda and Zimbabwe more than half of female sex workers are living with HIV.[23]

Although the number of new HIV infections among sex workers in 2014 was lower than among men who have sex with men in the region, the substantial (but undocumented) number of clients of sex workers who are exposed to HIV means HIV among this key population group has the greatest impact on the region's epidemic overall.[24]

It is estimated that at least 90% of sex workers in the region are female, although selling sex is also common among men who have sex with men and transgender people.[25] The majority of the region's countries identify sex workers in their national HIV strategies.[26] Despite this, how many sex workers are being reached with prevention and treatment is difficult to determine due to a lack of reported data.[27]

Condom usage by sex workers and their clients varies greatly. In some cases, sex workers have no access to condoms or are unaware of their importance. In other cases, police actively confiscate or destroy sex workers' condoms. A 2012 study in Kenya, South Africa and Zimbabwe found evidence of physical and sexual abuse and harassment of sex workers who carry condoms. Police were also using the threat of arrest on the grounds of condom possession to extort and exploit sex workers.[28]

Modelling estimates in Kenya show that a reduction of approximately 25% of HIV infections among sex workers may be achieved when physical or sexual violence is reduced.[29]

Men who have sex with men (MSM) and HIV in East and Southern Africa

While data on men who have sex with men (sometimes referred to as MSM) in East and Southern Africa is limited, HIV prevalence ranges from 3.8% in Angola to 36% in South Africa. Overall, one in three men who have sex with men is living with HIV in the region.[30]

HIV transmission between men who have sex with men accounted for 6% of new infections in the region in 2014.[31] However, evidence suggests the majority of the region's men who have sex with men also engage in heterosexual sex, often with wives or other long-term female partners.[32] The HIV epidemic among men who have sex with men is therefore interlaced with the epidemic in the wider population.[33]

Although limited, data reported between 2011 and 2015 suggest condom use exceeded 70% in South Africa, Kenya and Rwanda, and was above 50% in Comoros, Lesotho, Madagascar and Mauritius. eSwatini, Uganda and Tanzania reported levels below 50% at 46%, 39% and 14% respectively.[34]

The vast majority of national AIDS plans or strategies in the region identify men who have sex with men as a key population. However, specific programmes for this group are extremely limited and constrained by widespread homophobia and, in some countries, the criminalisation of same-sex practices.[35]

[...]

HIV testing and counselling (HTC) in East and Southern Africa

In recent years, a number of countries in the region such as Botswana, Kenya, Uganda, Malawi and Rwanda have implemented national campaigns to encourage uptake of HIV testing and counselling (HTC). In 2016, 76% of people living with HIV had knowledge about their status—an improvement from 72% in 2015.[45]

Access to HTC has been a major barrier to testing up-take and a number of strategies have been used to address this. Provider-initiated testing remains the region's main approach, but community-based testing is growing as it has been shown to be effective in reaching large numbers of first-time testers, diagnosing people living with HIV at earlier stages of infection, and linking those who test positive to care. Workplace and door-to-door testing, using rapid diagnostic tests, is also increasing.[46]

HIV-related stigma remains a huge barrier to testing, something that self-testing kits may help to side-step. In 2015, Kenya announced plans to introduce self-test kits.[47] In the same year, self-testing began in Malawi, Zambia and Zimbabwe through the four-year STAR (Self-Testing Africa Research) Project. By 2017, the STAR Project had distributed nearly 750,000 self-test kits across the three countries.[48]

Evidence from STAR suggests that, when provided as part of a community-based approach, self-testing is increasing HIV testing among men and adolescents in the region, groups that have been previously hard to reach. It has also been shown to improve the proportion of key populations testing positive who then access treatment.[49]

[...]

HIV prevention programmes in East and Southern Africa

In 2016, around 790,000 people in East and Southern Africa were newly infected with HIV.[51]

A number of countries in the region have conducted large-scale prevention programmes in an effort to contain and reduce their HIV epidemics. In 2015, Ethiopia, Malawi, eSwatini and Zimbabwe looked at how to revitalise their national prevention programmes. In the same year, government representatives of Kenya, Zimbabwe and South Africa met to plan the development of a regional roadmap to accelerate scale-up of combination HIV prevention services at local levels and increase investments for combination HIV prevention.[52]

Programmes for young women

In 2013 ministers of health and education from countries across the region committed to bringing in a raft of programmes to address the barriers that prevent girls and young women from accessing services. Focuses include keeping girls in school, comprehensive sexuality education, girl-friendly sexual and reproductive health services, eliminating gender-based violence and female genital mutilation, and economic and political empowerment.[53]

[…]

Condom availability and use

Condom availability varies widely by country, with only five countries meeting the United Nations Population Fund (UNFPA) regional benchmark of 30 male condoms distributed per man per year between 2011 and 2014.[56]

Condom use at last sex among adults with more than one sexual partner in the past 12 months is low, estimated at 23% among men and 33% among women. There is substantial variation among countries, ranging from 7% among men in Madagascar to 83% among men in eSwatini. Condom use among men who pay for sex is higher, at about 60%.[57]

HIV education and approach to sex education in East and Southern Africa

In 2013, 20 countries in the region committed to improving sexual and reproductive education for young people. By 2015, 14 were providing comprehensive sexuality education (CSE) and life skills in at least 40% of primary schools; 15 were providing CSE/life skills in at least 40% of secondary schools; and 18 were including sexual and reproductive health (SRH) and CSE training for people training to be teachers.[58]

A number of HIV prevention awareness campaigns targeting adults have also proven successful including the multi-country One Love campaign and South Africa's Love-Life.[59]

Prevention of mother-to-child transmission (PMTCT) in East and Southern Africa

Significant progress has been made in the prevention of mother-to-child transmission (PMTCT) of HIV in East and Southern Africa.

Between 2010 and 2015, new HIV infections declined by 66% among children (0–14 years) to an estimated 56,000.[60] However, in 2016 this rose to 77,000.[61]

The general decline in infections is due to the rapid increase in PMTCT services, from 61% coverage in 2010 to 89% in 2016. This equates to 854,000 pregnant women who are living with HIV on antiretroviral treatment (ART) in the region.[62]

In 2016, Botswana, Namibia, South Africa, eSwatini and Uganda had PMTCT coverage above 95%, Zimbabwe had 93% coverage, and Kenya, Mozambique, Rwanda, Malawi, Tanzania and Zambia had coverage of 80% or above. At the other end of the scale, Madagascar had just 3% coverage, South Sudan had 29% coverage, and Angola and Eritrea had coverage of around 40%.[63]

[…]

References
1. UNAIDS 'AIDSinfo' [Accessed 14/09/2017]
2. UNAIDS (2017) 'Data Book'
3. UNAIDS 'AIDSinfo' [Accessed 14/09/2017]
4. UNAIDS (2017) 'Ending AIDS: Progress towards 90-90-90 targets'
5. UNAIDS (2017) 'Ending AIDS: Progress towards 90-90-90 targets'
6. UNAIDS 'AIDSinfo' [Accessed 14/09/2017]
7. UNAIDS (2017) 'Ending AIDS: Progress towards the 90–90–90 targets'
8. UNAIDS (2017) 'UNAIDS DATA 2017' In 2016, 25% of new HIV infections in sub-Saharan Africa (no data available specifically for East and Southern Africa) were among key affected populations and their sexual partners, despite these

groups making up a fraction of the total population. Yet programming for key populations remains insufficient and many people from these groups face stigma, discrimination and legal barriers that prevent them from accessing HIV services. UNAIDS (2017) 'Ending AIDS: Progress towards the 90–90–90 targets'

9. UNAIDS 'AIDSinfo' [Accessed 14/09/2017]
10. United Nations Children's Fund (2015) 'Synthesis report of the rapid assessment of adolescent and HIV programme in five countries: Botswana, Cameroon, Jamaica, Swaziland and Zimbabwe'
11. Schaefer R., Gregson S., Eaton JW., Mugurungi O., Rhead R., Takaruza A., Maswera R., Nyamukapa C. (2017) 'Age-disparate relationships and HIV incidence in adolescent girls and young women: evidence from Zimbabwe'
12. UNAIDS (2014) 'The Gap Report'
13. Jewkes RK., Dunkle K., Nduna M., Shai N (2010) 'Intimate partner violence, relationship power inequity and incidence of HIV infection in young women in South Africa: a cohort study' Lancet. 2010;376(9734):41–48
14. UNAIDS (2016) 'Prevention Gap Report'
15. UNAIDS/UNICEF (2016) 'All in to end adolescent AIDS: A progress report'
16. UNAIDS (2017) 'Ending AIDS: Progress towards the 90–90–90 targets'
23. UNAIDS (2017) 'Towards ending AIDS in Eastern and Southern Africa Region: Leaving no one behind'
24. ibid
25. UNAIDS (2017) 'Towards ending AIDS in Eastern and Southern Africa Region: Leaving no one behind'
26. UNAIDS (2016) 'Prevention Gap Report'
27. UNAIDS (2013) 'Getting to zero: HIV in eastern and southern Africa'
28. The Open Society Foundation (2012) 'How Policing Practices Put Sex Workers and HIV Services at Risk in Kenya, Namibia, Russia, South Africa, the United States, and Zimbabwe'
29. Decker MR, et al. (2013) 'Estimating the impact of reducing violence against female sex workers on HIV epidemics in Kenya and Ukraine: a policy modeling exercise' Am J Reprod Immunol, 69 Suppl1:122–132
30. UNAIDS (2017) 'Towards ending AIDS in Eastern and Southern Africa Region: Leaving no one behind'
31. ibid
32. For example, see: Beyrer C., Trapence G., Motimedi F., Umar E., Iipinge S., Dausab F., et al. (2010) 'Bisexual concurrency, bisexual partnerships, and HIV among Southern African men who have sex with men' Sexually Transmitted Infections, 86(4):323–327 and Broz D., Okal J., Tun W., Sheehy M., Mutua M., Muraguri N., et al. (2011) 'High levels of bisexual behaviors among men who have sex with men in Nairobi, Kenya' ,6th IAS Conference on HIV Pathogenesis, Treatment and Prevention Rome, Italy, July 17–20, 2011, Abstract no MOLBPE046
33. UNAIDS (2013) 'Getting to zero: HIV in eastern and southern Africa'
34. UNAIDS (2017) 'UNAIDS DATA 2017'
35. UNAIDS (2016) 'Prevention Gap Report'
45. UNAIDS (2017) 'Ending AIDS: Progress towards 90-90-90 targets'
46. UNAIDS (2017) 'Ending AIDS: Progress towards 90-90-90 targets'
47. UNAIDS (2016) 'Prevention Gap Report'
48. UNAIDS (2017) 'Ending AIDS: Progress towards 90-90-90 targets'
49. ibid
51. UNAIDS (2017) 'UNAIDS DATA 2017'

52. UNAIDS (2016) 'Prevention Gap Report'
53. UNAIDS (2016) 'Prevention Gap Report'
56. UNAIDS (2016) 'Prevention Gap Report'
57. UNAIDS (2016) 'Prevention Gap Report'
58. Young People Today 'Regional progress 2015: target highlights' (Accessed 11/01/2018)
59. UNAIDS (2016) 'Prevention Gap Report'
60. UNAIDS (2016) 'Prevention Gap Report'
61. UNAIDS 'East and Southern Africa: Data 2016' (Accessed 10/01/2018)
62. UNAIDS 'AIDSinfo' (Accessed 11/01/2018)
63. UNAIDS (2017) 'UNAIDS DATA 2017'

In France Expansion of Access to Reproductive Health Services Should Pave the Way for Women Around the World to Control Their Own Bodies

Rebecca Brown

In the following viewpoint, Rebecca Brown details the 2014 change France made to its abortion laws, ensuring that a woman has a legal right to an abortion through the first twelve weeks of pregnancy and criminalizes attempts to obstruct that right. It is a stride made at the tail end of the deadline of the United Nations' Millennium Development Goals, which is a benchmark of goals to meet by 2015. Since the MDGs went into effect, 222 million women who want to avoid or delay pregnancy still are unable to obtain modern contraception in developing countries, and in sixty-six countries around the world abortion is either illegal or heavily restricted. Brown is director of global advocacy at the Center for Reproductive Rights.

"Women Must Have Control Over Their Own Bodies," by Rebecca Brown, PassBlue, March 9, 2014. Reprinted by permission.

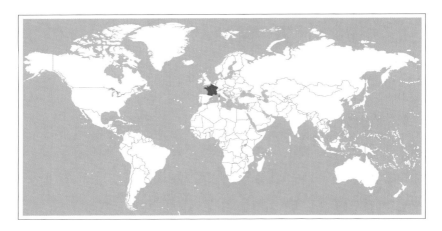

As you read, consider the following questions:

1. Should attempts to obstruct a woman's right to have a safe and sanitary abortion be criminalized? Why or why not?
2. How do reproductive rights violations reinforce discrimination, poverty, and violence?
3. How does France's abortion law advance equality between genders in that country?

Earlier this year France was the latest to join a handful of progressive countries to expand access to reproductive health services—with its National Assembly amending the country's laws to affirm a woman's right to an abortion through the first 12 weeks of pregnancy and criminalize attempts to obstruct this right.

What is refreshing about this amendment to the French abortion law is that it was not standalone legislation but part of the Real Equality Between Men and Women bill, a package of measures to address gender inequality. Besides ensuring women's access to reproductive health care, the legislation includes extending paternity leave to six months, banning beauty contests for girls under 13 years old and imposing higher fines on businesses and political parties that fail to respect gender parity.

France's concrete steps are exactly what the United Nations should be doing over the next 10 days, as delegates from the UN, other government representatives and civil society members gather in New York for the 58th session of the UN Commission on the Status of Women, an annual conference to assess the condition of women worldwide.

The theme of this year's conference, held March 10-21, will concentrate on implementation of the Millennium Development Goals—the UN blueprint for eradicating poverty, hunger and disease—for women and girls, which will inform the new development agenda starting in 2015, when the current goals end.

When the UN and member states negotiated the Millennium Development Goals (MDGs), they set out to improve access to maternal health care and later to a broader range of reproductive health services as well as to promote gender equality. The MDGs treat the two aims separately when they are clearly interrelated.

It has become abundantly clear since the MDGs were established in 2000 and are now winding up, that first and foremost, women can be equal in society only if they can freely decide the number and spacing of their children. Achieving equality, particularly gender equality, has also been articulated as one of the main goals of both international development programs and international human rights law.

Development programs, however, have had limited success so far in eliminating the root causes of inequalities that women face, which in turn hinder the realization of women's rights. We see this explicitly with reproductive rights.

Fourteen years after the Millennium Development Goals went into effect, 222 million women who want to avoid or delay pregnancy still cannot obtain modern contraception in developing nations. In 66 countries, abortion is either prohibited in all circumstances or allowed only to save a woman's life. Women in these circumstances have virtually no control over the size of their families—a serious problem that carries over to other important

Trump's Opposition to Breastfeeding

Advocates for improved nutrition for babies have expressed outrage over reports that the Trump administration bullied other governments in an attempt to prevent the passage of an international resolution promoting breastfeeding.

The US delegation to the World Health Assembly in Geneva reportedly deployed threats and other heavy-handed measures to try to browbeat nations into backing off the resolution.

Under the terms of the original WHO text, countries would have encouraged their citizens to breastfeed on grounds that research overwhelmingly shows its health benefits, while warning parents to be alert to inaccurate marketing by formula milk firms.

The New York Times first reported how the Trump administration reacted forcefully to the resolution, which otherwise had the consensus support of all other assembly members. It pushed to remove a phrase from the draft text that would exhort governments to "protect, promote and support breast-feeding".

The administration also used its network of diplomats to lean on member states. Turning on the delegation from Ecuador, the US government said that unless the South American nation withdrew its backing of the resolution it would face punitive trade moves and even the potential loss of military help in its battle against gang violence.

decisions they must make about their lives, like their education or employment.

International human-rights norms recognize that reproductive rights violations often stem from, as well as reinforce, discrimination, poverty and violence. International human-rights treaties make clear that ensuring gender equality, including its reproductive rights aspects, is a human-rights obligation that states must respect, protect and fulfill.

Last year, 131 countries at the Commission on the Status of Women agreed to adopt a plan to combat violence against women and girls, urging all countries "to strongly condemn all forms of violence against women and girls and to refrain from invoking

The resolution was eventually passed with US support, but only after the Russian government reintroduced it using a modified text.

Lucy Sullivan, executive director of 1,000 Days, the US-headquartered international group working to improve nutrition for babies and infants, said in a Twitter thread that the US intervention amounted to "public health versus private profit. What is at stake: breastfeeding saves women and children's lives. It is also bad for the multibillion-dollar global infant formula (and dairy) business."

The online network of mothers, Moms Rising, called the US government's move "stunning and shameful. We must do everything we can to advocate for public policies that support and empower breastfeeding moms."

Patti Rundall of the UK-based campaign Baby Milk Action told the New York Times: "We were astonished, appalled and also saddened. What happened was tantamount to blackmail, with the US holding the world hostage and trying to overturn nearly 40 years of consensus on the best way to protect infant and young child health."

Under an internal code of the World Health Organisation, baby formula companies are banned from explicitly targeting mothers and their health carers. Advertising is also controlled.

"Trump administration's opposition to breastfeeding resolution sparks outrage," by Ed Pilkington, July 8, 2018.

any custom, tradition, and religious consideration to avoid their obligations with respect to its elimination."

As the principal global policy-making body dedicated exclusively to gender equality and the advancement of women, the commission now must address another barrier to gender equality—by calling on countries to ensure that all women can fully exercise their reproductive rights.

Over the next two years, countries have an opportunity to focus on the root causes of gender inequality by insisting that reproductive rights, the need to ensure equal access to health care services and opportunities for women are embedded throughout the post-2015 agenda, including under the likely goals related to gender equality, health, education and accountability/governance, which will be adopted by the end of 2015.

Women's reproductive rights lie at the heart of their basic human rights. The UN and governments must adopt and enforce laws and policies that allow all women to control their fertility, their health and their lives.

In the United States the Unintended Teen Pregnancy Rate Is Among the Highest in Developing Nations

Emily Bridges

In the following viewpoint, Emily Bridges writes about the research being done on programs used in schools, communities, and clinics that can help teens prevent pregnancy. Important hallmarks of these programs include educating teens on the importance of abstaining from pregnancy but also the use of contraceptives and condoms for teens who make the decision to participate in sexual activity. In 2006, the US teen pregnancy rate was 71.5 pregnancies per 1000 women ages fifteen to nineteen, a significant decline from the rate of 116.9 pregnancies per 1000 in 1990. While teen pregnancy rates are dropping in the United States, they are still among the highest in developing nations. Bridges is Advocates for Youth's director of communications.

As you read, consider the following questions:

1. Per the viewpoint, why do young women in their twenties have the highest abortion rates of any group?
2. What accounts for the decline in unintended teen pregnancies in the United States?
3. What are the best ways to ensure the prevention of unintended teen pregnancy and keep teens from the "cycle of poverty"? How can they be established?

"Unintended Pregnancy Among Young People in the United States", by Emily Bridges, Advocates for Youth, October 2011. Reprinted by permission.

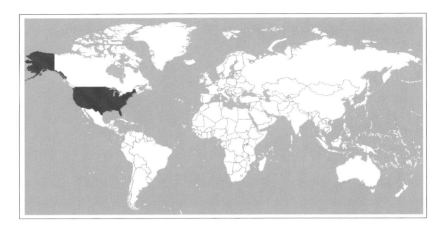

L argely due to increased contraceptive use, teen pregnancy
and birth rates have declined since their peak in 1990. [1]
But 750,000 teens become pregnant each year—the vast majority
(82 percent) of these pregnancies unintended. [2,3] Teens need
youth-friendly services and complete, accurate information about
abstinence, condoms, and contraception in order to protect
themselves from unintended pregnancy. But they also need to
be able to envision a positive future for themselves: one in which
education, employment, and healthy relationships are possible.
Helping young people prevent unintended pregnancy is a challenge
that teens, parents, youth serving professionals, policy makers,
and society as a whole must face.

U.S. Teen Pregnancy, Birth, and Abortion Rates Have Declined Overall, but Are Still Higher Than Those in Many Industrialized Nations

In 2006, the most recent year for which information is available,
the estimated U.S. teen pregnancy rate was 71.5 pregnancies per
1,000 young women ages 15 to 19. The rate rose slightly from
69.5 between 2005–2006 (with a decline in teen contraceptive
use as one possible explanation). [2,4] But overall, the rate has
dropped significantly (39 percent) since 1990 when it peaked at
a rate of 116.9. [2]

The birth rate for teens ages 15–19 has fluctuated slightly in recent years, but in 2009, fell to its lowest point ever, of 39.1 births per 1000 young women ages 15–19. Overall, the rate has declined 35 percent since its peak in 1990. In 2009, 409,840 teens gave birth. [5,6]

In 2007, among young women 15–19, 14.5 out of every 1000 obtained an abortion. The teen abortion rate has fallen by 25 percent since 1998. [7]

By comparison, the United States' teen pregnancy rate is over four times that of the Netherlands (14.1) over three times that of Germany (18.8), and almost three times that of France (25.7). The United States' teen birth rate is nearly eight times higher than that of the Netherlands' (5.3), over five times higher than France's (7.1), and over four times higher than Germany's (9.6). [2,8,9]

Older Teens Account for The Majority of Teen Pregnancies, Births, And Abortions – but Many Thousands of Younger Teens Are Affected

The pregnancy rate among teens ages 15–17 was 38.9 in 2006, with teens in this age group experiencing a little under a third of the total number of teen pregnancies. The pregnancy rate among teens ages 18–19 was 122.3 in 2006, with teens in this age group experiencing two thirds of the total number of teen pregnancies. [2]

The birth rate among teens ages 15–17 was 20.1 in 2009; over 117,000 teens ages 15–17 gave birth. The birth rate among teens ages 18–19 was 66.2 births per 1000 teens; over 240,000 teens ages 18–19 gave birth. Over a thousand youth under the age of 14 gave birth. [6]

Like the pregnancy and birth rates, the abortion rate among teens rises as teens age. The abortion rate for fifteen year olds is 4.6 abortions per 1000 young women; for 16 year olds, 8.6; 17 year olds, 13.0; 18 year olds, 21.9; and 19 year olds, 26.7.

Young Women in Their Twenties Experience Many Unintended Pregnancies

One-third of all unintended pregnancies are to young women in their twenties. Eighty-six percent of pregnancies among unmarried women in their twenties are unplanned. [10]

Women in their twenties account for 57 percent of abortions in the U.S and have the highest abortion rates of any age group: 29.4 abortions per 1,000 women aged 20–24 years and 21.4 abortions per 1,000 women aged 25–29 years. [7]

Unintended pregnancy among young women in their twenties affects women of all races, education levels, and income levels. [10]

Youth of Color Experience Pregnancy and Birth At Disproportionate Rates, While Whites Account for The Highest Numbers

Teen pregnancy rates have declined to varying degrees among racial/ethnic groups. Since 1990, for young women ages 15–19, the pregnancy rate has declined 44 percent for African Americans, 22 percent for Hispanics, 56 percent for Asians/Pacific Islanders, and 38 percent for whites. [2,5]

Among races/ethnicities, young white women experience the majority of pregnancies and births. Young white women ages 15–19 experienced just under 279,000 pregnancies in 2006, compared to 206,000 among African Americans and 209,000 among Hispanics.2 In 2009, 159,526 young white women ages 15–19 gave birth, compared to 98,425 African Americans and 136,274 Hispanics. [6]

African American and Hispanic teens are more than twice as likely to experience pregnancy as white teens. Per 1000 young women ages 15–19 in 2006, 126.3 African Americans became pregnant and 126.6 Hispanics became pregnant compared to 61.1 whites. [2]

Drop in Teen Pregnancy

Teen pregnancy is way down. And a study suggests that the reason is increased, and increasingly effective, use of contraceptives.

From 2007 to 2013, births to teens age 15 to 19 dropped by 36 percent; pregnancies fell by 25 percent from 2007 to 2011, according to federal data.

But that wasn't because teens were shunning sex. The amount of sex being had by teenagers during that time period was largely unchanged, says the study, which was published online in the Journal of Adolescent Health. And it wasn't because they were having more abortions. Abortion has been declining among all age groups, and particularly among teenagers.

Rather, the researchers from the Guttmacher Institute and Columbia University found that "improvement in contraceptive use" accounted for the entire reduced risk of pregnancy over the five-year period. No single contraceptive method stood out as singularly effective, said the researchers. Instead, they found that teens were using contraceptives more often, combining methods more often, and using more effective methods, such as the birth control pill, IUDs and implants.

Also, the use of any contraceptive at all makes a big difference, said Lindberg. "If a teen uses no method they have an 85 percent chance of getting pregnant [within a year]. Using anything is way more effective than that 85 percent risk."

The downturn in teen births actually dates back to the early 1990s, the authors say, with the rate dropping by 57 percent between 1991 and 2013. The increase in contraceptive use dates to the mid-1990s, with the use of any contraceptive at the most recent sexual encounter rising from 66 to 86 percent from 1995 to 2012.

More recent policy changes could help drop the teen pregnancy rate even more. One is the Affordable Care Act requirement that boosted insurance coverage for contraception, starting in 2012. The other is the 2014 recommendation from the American Academy of Pediatrics that sexually active teenagers be offered "long-acting reversible contraception" methods such as implants and intrauterine devices, which are highly effective and do not require any additional action, such as remembering to take a daily pill.

"Drop In Teen Pregnancies Is Due To More Contraceptives, Not Less Sex", by Julie Rovner, Henry J. Kaiser Family Foundation, August 31, 2016. Reprinted by permission.

Teens of color are also more than twice as likely to give birth as white teens. Per 1000 young women ages 15–19 in 2009, 59 African Americans gave birth, 70.1 Hispanics gave birth, and 55.5 American Indian/Alaska Natives gave birth compared to 25.6 whites. [6]

Among young women in their twenties, whites experienced 44 percent of unintended pregnancies, African Americans 32 percent, and Hispanics 19 percent. [10]

Teen Pregnancy and Birth Create Barriers to Success for Teens and Their Children

Young women who are teen mothers are less likely to attain a high school diploma by age 22 than those who are not (fifty-one percent compared to 89 percent). [11]

Less than two percent of teen mothers complete college by age 30. [12]

When earnings are compared over the first 15 years of motherhood, women who were teen mothers earn significantly less than women who were not. Teen mothers are also more likely to be on welfare. [14]

Teen parents are at risk of subsequent pregnancy: over one fifth of births to teens in the U.S. are second births. [13] About one-fourth of teenage mothers have a second child within two years of their first birth. [14] Subsequent pregnancies can compound educational and financial difficulties for young women.

Children of teen mothers are more likely to be born prematurely and/or at low birth weight than children of older mothers, placing them at higher risk for other health problems. [15]

Approaches to Preventing Unintended Pregnancy Among Young People Must Include Dismantling Structural Barriers

Barriers to contraceptive access, poverty, and structural exclusion and disadvantage all contribute to young people's ability and motivation to prevent unintended pregnancy.

Among teens, pregnancy is both a cause and a result of poverty and low academic achievement. Teen pregnancy is part of the "cycle of poverty" in which very young mothers often stay poor, and their children are at increased risk for teen pregnancy, poverty, and lower academic outcomes. [16]

Teens are more likely to become pregnant as teens if their mother or sister gives birth as a teen, or if teen pregnancy is common in their community. [17]

Teens who have low expectations for their futures or feel that they lack control over their lives are more likely to experience pregnancy. [18]

Teen pregnancy can also be impacted by immigration status. For instance, Latino immigrant youth have lower rates of sexual activity and later sexual debut than non-immigrant children, but also fewer resources for obtaining quality health care and education; they subsequently have higher teen pregnancy rates than white youth. [19]

Young people face many challenges to sexual health beyond pregnancy (including STIs and HIV, unhealthy relationships, developing sexuality, and mental health issues). In addition to helping young people prevent pregnancy, society must ensure their environment as a whole fosters reproductive and sexual health – including full access to health care, health information, and educational opportunities. [19]

Empowering youth, and supporting women's reproductive decisions, means young people who become mothers should be supported, not stigmatized, by both government and culture. [19]

Conclusion

Research has identified a number of effective programs for use in schools, communities, and clinics which can help teens prevent pregnancy. These programs share certain characteristics: they provide instruction on abstinence as well as contraception and condoms; they are age-appropriate and culturally competent; and they help teens build the specific skills they need to protect themselves. [20,21] In addition, open and honest parent-child communication about sex, sexuality, and relationships helps teens lower their risk behaviors and increase their use of contraception. [22,23,24,25,26] But along with behavioral interventions, advocates should support structural interventions, including: redressing socioeconomic disparities that contribute to teen pregnancy; improving youth access to confidential contraception and other health services; and supporting youth development strategies that enhance young people's sense of empowerment and control and deepen connections to family and school.

Notes

1. Santelli, J. Explaining Recent Declines in Adolescent Pregnancy in the United States: The Contribution of Abstinence and Improved Contraceptive Use. American Journal of Public Health, January 2007: 97:1.
2. Kost K, et al U.S. Teenage pregnancies, births and abortions: National and state trends and trends by race and ethnicity. Guttmacher Institute 2010.
3. Finer LB et al., Disparities in rates of unintended pregnancy in the United States, 1994 and 2001, Perspectives on Sexual and Reproductive Health, 2006, 38(2):90–96.
4. Santelli J et al. Changing Behavioral Risk for Pregnancy Among High School Students in the United States, 1991–2007. Journal of Adolescent Health 2009: 45(1).
5. Ventura SJ, Hamilton BE. U.S. teenage birth rate resumes decline. NCHS data brief, no 58. Hyattsville, MD: National Center for Health Statistics. 2011.
6. Hamilton, B. E., Martin, J. A., and Ventura, S. J. (2010). Births: Preliminary data for 2009. National Vital Statistics Reports, 59 (3). http://www.cdc.gov/nchs/data/nvsr/nvsr59/nvsr59_03.pdf. Accessed 3/8/2011.
7. Pazol K et al. Abortion Surveillance – United States, 2007. MMWR Surveillance Summaries, 20011: 60(1). http://www.cdc.gov/mmwr/preview/mmwrhtml/ss6001a1.htm?s_cid=ss6001a1_w . Accessed 3/8/2011.
8. Henshaw S. Personal Communication. Guttmacher Institute, October 31, 2007.
9. Lee, Laura, van, Ineke van der Vlucht, Ciel Wijsen, and FrankaCadée. 2009. Fact Sheet 2009: Tienerzwangerschappen,abortus en tienermoeders in Nederland: Feiten en Cijfers. Utrecht: Rutgers Nisso Groep.
10. The National Campaign to Prevent Teen and Unplanned Pregnancy. "Unplanned Pregnancy Among 20-somethings: The Full Story." May 2008, The National Campaign. Accessed from http://www.thenationalcampaign.org/resources/pdf/briefly-unplanned-pregnancy-among-20somethings-the-full-story.pdf on October 3, 2011.
11. Perper K, Peterson K, Manlove J. Diploma attainment among teen mothers. Child Trends, Washington, DC: 2010.
12. Hoffman, S.D., By the Numbers: The Public Costs of Adolescent Childbearing. 2006, The National Campaign to Prevent Teen Pregnancy Washington, DC.
13. Manlove J, Mariner C, & Papillo AR, Subsequent fertility among teen mothers: Longitudinal analyses of recent national data, Journal of Marriage & the Family, 2000, 62(2): 430-448.

14. Kalmuss, D.S., & Namerow, P.B., Subsequent childbearing among teenage mothers: The determinants of closely spaced second birth. Family Planning Perspectives, 1994. 26(4): p. 149-153.
15. Martin, J.A., Hamilton, B.E., Ventura, S.J., Menacker, F. & Kirmeyer, S., Births: Final Data for 2004. National Vital Statistics Reports, 2006. 55(1).
16. Basch CE. Healthier Students Are Better Learners: a Missing Link in School Reforms to Close the Achievement Gap. [Equity Matters; Research Review #6]. NY: Teachers College of Columbia University, 2010.
17. Coley RL, Chase-Lansdale PL. Adolescent pregnancy and parenthood: recent evidence and future directions. American Psychologist. 1998; 53:152–166.
18. Harden A. Teenage pregnancy and social disadvantage: systematic review integrating controlled trials and qualitative studies. BMJ 2009; 339.
19. Fuentes L, Bayetti Flores V, Gonzalez-Rojas J. Removing Stigma: Towards a Complete Understanding of Young Latinas' Sexual Health, New York: National Latina Institute for Reproductive Health, 2010.
20. Kirby D. Emerging Answers 2007. Washington, DC: National Campaign to Prevent Teen Pregnancy, 2007.
21. Alford S et al. Science and Success: Sex Education and Other Programs that Work to Prevent Teen Pregnancy, HIV & Sexually Transmitted Infections. 2nd Edition. Washington, DC: Advocates for Youth, 2008
22. Weinman M, Small E, Buzi RS, Smith P. Risk Factors, Parental Communication, Self and Peers' Beliefs as Predictors of Condom Use Among Female Adolescents Attending Family Planning Clinics. Child Adolesc Soc Work J 2008;25:157-170.
23. Miller KS et al. Patterns of condom use among adolescents: the impact of mother-adolescent communication. Am J Public Health1998;88:1542-44.
24. Hacker KA et al. Listening to youth: teen perspectives on pregnancy prevention. J Adolesc Health 2000;26:279-88.
25. Jemmott LS, Jemmott JB. Family structure, parental strictness, and sexual behavior among inner-city black male adolescents. J Adolesc Research 1992; 7:192-207.
26. Rodgers KB. Parenting processes related to sexual risk-taking behaviors of adolescent males and females. J Marriage Fam 1999;61:99-109.]

Sexuality and Reproductive Health After Giving Birth

Family Planning NSW

In the following viewpoint, writers from Family Planning NSW detail the sexual and reproductive issues that new mothers can face after giving birth. For many women, it takes six weeks or longer to recover from the damage caused by giving birth. At this time, a woman can experience heavy bleeding, not dissimilar to a menstrual period, but it can last much longer. Additionally, whether they choose to have intercourse or not, women who do not want to get pregnant so soon after giving birth should use contraception, including the progestogen-only pill, the implant, and the DMPA injection, which can be administered immediately after birth. Family Planning NSW is a nonprofit provider of reproductive and sexual health services in Australia.

As you read, consider the following questions:

1. What are the changes a woman's body undergoes after giving birth?
2. Why is contraception important for a woman after giving birth?
3. How many women experience postnatal "baby blues" and why is it important to destigmatize the issue and seek treatment?

Family Planning NSW. After having a baby: sexuality and reproductive health [online] 2014. https://www.fpnsw.org.au/health-information/individuals/pregnancy/after-having-baby-sexuality-and-reproductive-health. Reprinted by permission.

A woman's body goes through enormous change after giving birth and in the weeks that follow. The terms "post-partum"and "post-natal" refer to the period of time immediately after giving birth, and for the next six weeks.

Over this time the body is returning back to the non-pregnant state; however this does not mean that women can expect to feel "back to normal" after 6 weeks—for some women it can take much longer than this. It is recommended to have a post-natal check-up with a GP or family planning clinic when the baby is about 6 weeks old, which can help identify any issues and provide an opportunity to discuss any concerns.

It is also a good opportunity to discuss contraception, if this hasn't been addressed already.

Bleeding (lochia)

The vaginal bleeding that women experience after giving birth is referred to as "lochia." This gradually decreases over the 4–6 weeks after delivery, and often becomes a pink or brown colour.

If a woman is not breastfeeding, the first period may occur as soon as 4 weeks after giving birth.

For women who are breastfeeding, the average time for periods to return is 28 weeks after delivery; however there is a wide range around this average.

Contraception

Contraception is advised from day 21 post-partum onwards in women who are not breastfeeding and who wish to avoid another pregnancy. All of the hormonal methods of contraception that are available in Australia are generally suitable for use from day 21 onwards in women who are not breastfeeding, with the exception of IUDs, which are recommended to be inserted either within the first 48 hours of delivery, or from 4–8 weeks post-partum.

The progestogen-only pill, the implant and the injection (DMPA) can also be started immediately after delivery. For breastfeeding women, the lactational amenorrhoea method (LAM) can be used for the first six months after delivery, provided the woman's periods have not returned, and the baby is fully breastfed with no long intervals between day or night feeds, and not given any supplements other than infrequent vitamins, water or juice.

If all of these criteria are fulfilled, LAM is 98% effective (i.e., for 100 women using this method correctly, 2 will become pregnant). However a woman can ovulate before her periods return so breastfeeding women are usually recommended to use an additional method of contraception if they wish to avoid pregnancy.

Contraceptive options for women who are breastfeeding are the progestogen-only pill, the injection, and the implant, with IUDs again being available within the first 48 hours or after 4–8 weeks post-partum. The combined pill and vaginal ring can be used by most breastfeeding women whose babies are older than 6 months.

Post-partum sexuality

Following the birth of a child, there is wide variation in the time when a woman feels ready to resume sexual activity. Some women report a return of sexual desire within 2–3 weeks, but many others will experience delays lasting from weeks to many months.

There are many factors which can contribute to this. Firstly there may be bruising or swelling of the vulva and vagina following delivery, and if the woman required stitches for an episiotomy or a perineal tear, this area can remain tender for some months.

This can cause pain on penetration, so it can be advisable to try other forms of sexual activity which do not require vaginal penetration until the area has completely healed. The hormonal changes that occur after giving birth can also contribute to pain or discomfort during penetration.

The vagina often feels drier as well. This can last for 2–3 months in women who are not breastfeeding, but considerably longer in women who are breastfeeding. Water-based lubricants can be helpful, as can vaginal moisturisers, both available over the counter at a pharmacy.

If these measures are insufficient, it is worth talking to a doctor about whether oestrogen cream or pessaries may be a useful option.

Some women also experience an involuntary tightening of the vaginal muscles in response to attempted vaginal penetration. This is called vaginismus. This generally requires assessment and treatment by a physiotherapist who specialises in pelvic floor problems.

Pelvic floor exercises are recommended for all women during pregnancy and post-natally. Strengthening the pelvic floor muscles reduces the incidence of stress urinary incontinence (leaking urine when you cough, sneeze or exercise) and can also prevent prolapse (where your uterus, bladder or bowel sag into the vagina). Pelvic floor muscles are frequently stretched during pregnancy and childbirth, which can lead to reduced sensation during sex for both partners.

Pelvic floor exercises can help improve this.

In breastfeeding women, breast tenderness and sensitivity may mean a change in the usual pattern of arousal. It is normal for a letdown of milk to occur during arousal and orgasm. This may be prevented, if desired, by breastfeeding before sexual activity.

Tiredness, changing roles and relationships in the family, and particularly with your partner, and concerns about sexual attractiveness, can all have an effect on sexual desire and function.

These issues are all very common, but it may be useful to see a sex therapist or counsellor, either alone or as a couple, who can give more specialised help with these issues.

Post-natal depression

Up to 80% of women experience 'the baby blues' shortly after the birth of a baby. This is a normal process where the woman feels tearful, anxious, depressed and/or has mood swings in the first week after giving birth.

It is thought to be due to the stresses associated with labour and delivery, and the fluctuating hormone levels that occur after giving birth. These symptoms should settle within the first week of giving birth, and often support and rest is all that is required.

However if these symptoms continue beyond 2 weeks post-partum, or are severe, it may indicate post-natal depression.

Post-natal depression refers to severe or prolonged symptoms of depression that last for more than 2 weeks and have an impact on the ability to function with normal routines on a daily basis. Post-natal depression is a treatable illness and it is important to seek help from a GP.

Inequalities Stand in the Way of Achieving Reproductive Rights

Bjorn Andersson

In the following viewpoint Bjorn Andersson argues that gender, economic, racial, social, and sexual inequalities keep women around the world—particularly in developing nations—from advancing. Inequalities in reproductive rights hold women back because, without access to family planning, they can become mired in a cycle of poverty. Conversely, girls and women who are educated about family planning can complete their education, join the workforce, and contribute to society and their economies. The author implores governments to work together to improve the lives of women around the world. Andersson is Asia-Pacific regional director of the United Nations Population Fund.

As you read, consider the following questions:

1. How many babies were born to teenage mothers in Thailand over the last fifteen years?
2. What is SDG1 of the UN's goals according to the viewpoint?
3. What has Thailand's government done to help girls stay in school according to the author?

I n Bangkok's sprawling outer suburbs, the Emergency Home offers a secure haven, providing crisis care and shelter for

"Why reproductive rights are the first step to a freer, fairer world," by Bjorn Andersson, World Economic Forum, October 18, 2018. Reprinted by Permission.

adolescent and teenaged girls like Fern who find themselves unexpectedly pregnant, desperate and with nowhere else to go. Fern is 18, the youngest here is just 13, and the other residents fall somewhere in-between.

Although Thailand is classified as an upper middle-income country, with aspirations to reach fully developed status within the next 20 years, its teenage pregnancy statistics remain high. About 1.6 million babies were born to teenage mothers over the last 15 years, with a 54% increase from 2000 to 2014. In Thailand, as in so many countries across Asia and the Pacific, access to vital and comprehensive sex education at a young age is difficult, as is access to sexual and reproductive health services for young people.

Ten months ago, Mae Esparcia, 30, gave birth to her first child in Cavite, Philippines. After her delivery, Esparcia, a garment factory worker, decided to start using contraceptive pills, which she received for free from her workplace. Millions of other Filipino women would also like to plan the timing and the size of their families, but are unable to do so amid a sociocultural context long hostile to family planning, including modern contraception for which 18% of married women have an unmet need.

Access to contraception is improving globally—but at an ever-slower rate Access to contraception is improving globally—but at an ever-slower rate.

Many Dimensions of Inequality, Millions of Women Impacted

These are just two women whose stories, along with those of millions of others in Asia-Pacific and globally, illustrate how inequalities remain at the heart of the challenge to access and achieve optimal sexual and reproductive health and rights, especially for the most vulnerable and marginalised.

Economic disparities are only one aspect of inequality. Many other dimensions—social, racial, political, institutional—are in the mix, collectively blocking advancement for people on the margins.

Two such critical factors are gender inequality and inequalities in realising sexual and reproductive health and rights.

Unless we address these inequalities, many women and girls will remain mired in a vicious cycle of poverty, diminished capabilities, unfulfilled human rights and potential—not only in developing countries where gaps remain the widest, but in developed countries as well where deep pockets of inequality also persist.

For instance, typically the richest 20% have the greatest access to sexual and reproductive health care, and the poorest 20% have the least. Moreover, the poorest 20% of girls are nearly four times more likely to give birth between the ages of 15 and 19 in Asia-Pacific. Women in rural areas are three times more likely to die giving birth than women in urban areas, while 43% per cent of pregnancies in developing countries are unintended, with poorer, less-educated and rural women particularly at risk.

The World Economic Forum's global gender gap index captures differences between men and women in accessing resources and opportunities—for example, in income and labour-force participation, education, health and political empowerment. Of the 142 countries the index covered in 2016, 68 had larger gender gaps than the previous year. Inequalities in access to sexual and reproductive health and rights undeniably contribute to these gaps.

Three Messages, Three Steps

This year's flagship State of World Population Report from UNFPA, the United Nations Population Fund, spells all of this out very clearly. "Worlds Apart: Reproductive health and rights in an age of inequality" imparts three overarching messages backed up by irrefutable data.

First, unless we reduce inequalities in women's reproductive health and rights, the world will fail to achieve the UN's Sustainable Development Goals that underpin the 2030 Sustainable Development Agenda, and the most important goal, poverty reduction—SDG 1—will be blocked. When women are able to control their fertility, including by avoiding early marriage or unintended pregnancy, they can finish their education, enter the paid labour force and gain more economic power.

Second, we must heed the call of the SDGs to first reach those who are furthest behind if we are to realise shared prosperity. This can't happen without individuals and couples in the poorest segments of a country gaining access to reproductive health and family planning services. We need to prioritise adolescents, stop child or early marriage and prevent teen pregnancies. Countries with large youth populations can benefit from the "demographic dividend" through investing in education and delaying childbearing, to the benefit of future generations.

Third, we must implement a package of concrete actions that require governments to act together with civil society and, increasingly, in partnership with the private sector. These actions include tearing down barriers—discriminatory laws, norms or service gaps—that prevent adolescent girls and young women from accessing sexual and reproductive health information and services. The poorest women must be reached with essential, life-saving pregnancy, maternal and newborn healthcare. And all unmet demand for family planning must be met, prioritising the poorest women.

Periodical and Internet Sources Bibliography

The following articles have been selected to supplement the diverse views presented in this chapter.

African News Agency, "Brand South Africa calls on citizens to get tested for HIV," The Citizen, January 12, 2018. https://citizen.co.za/uncategorized/2044107/brand-south-africa-calls-on-citizens-to-get-tested-for-hiv/.

Rehka Basu, "Gov. Kim Reynolds should work to prevent unplanned pregnancies, not ban abortion," *Des Moines Register*, November 15, 2018. https://www.desmoinesregister.com/story/opinion/columnists/rekha-basu/2018/11/14/prevent-unwanted-pregnancy-outlaw-abortion-kim-reynolds-iowa-fetal-heartbeat-planned-parenthood/2003095002/.

Olivia Blair, "What Happens to Women's Bodies After Childbirth? Obstetrician Reveals All," *Independent*, February 23, 2017. https://www.independent.co.uk/life-style/health-and-families/womens-body-childbirth-impact-changes-obstetrician-reveals-pelvic-floor-bruising-bleeding-a7595031.html.

Sarah Bosley, "How Trump signed a global death warrant for women," *Guardian*, July 21, 2017. https://www.theguardian.com/global-development/2017/jul/21/trump-global-death-warrant-women-family-planning-population-reproductive-rights-mexico-city-policy.

Emily Dreyfuss, "Will Others Follow Microsoft's Lead on Paid Parental Leave?" *Wired*, August 31, 2018. https://www.wired.com/story/will-others-follow-microsoft-on-paid-parental-leave/.

Jill Filpovic, "America Will Lose More Than Abortion Rights If Roe v. Wade Is Overturned," *Time*, June 28, 2018. http://time.com/5324828/kennedy-retirement-roe-wade-abortion-rights/.

Barbara Gault, Heidi Hartmann, Ariane Hegewisch, Jessica Milli, Lindsey Reichlin, "Paid Parental Leave in the United States: What the Data Tell Us about Access, Usage, and Economic and Health Benefits," Institute for World Policy Research, January 23, 2014.

https://iwpr.org/publications/paid-parental-leave-in-the-united-states-what-the-data-tell-us-about-access-usage-and-economic-and-health-benefits/.

Rebecca Greenfield, "More Companies Than Ever Offer Paid Parental Leave," *Bloomberg*, June 28, 2018. https://www.bloomberg.com/news/articles/2018-06-28/more-companies-than-ever-offer-paid-parental-leave.

Shane Higgins, "The Psychology of Dealing with an Unplanned Pregnancy," Psych Central, 2013. https://psychcentral.com/blog/the-psychology-of-dealing-with-an-unplanned-pregnancy/.

Human Rights Watch, "Trump's 'Mexico City Policy' or 'Global Gag Rule'," Human Rights Watch, February 14, 2018. https://www.hrw.org/news/2018/02/14/trumps-mexico-city-policy-or-global-gag-rule.

Graça Machel & Erna Solberg, "We can end the epidemic in 13 years – but only if we fight on," *City Press*, December 1, 2018. https://city-press.news24.com/Voices/we-can-end-the-epidemic-in-13-years-but-only-if-we-fight-on-20181130.

Vaidehi Mujumdar, "The state still controls women's bodies. Especially brown and black ones," The Guardian, April 27, 2015. https://www.theguardian.com/commentisfree/2015/apr/27/the-state-still-controls-womens-bodies-especially-brown-and-black-ones.

Amy S. Patterson and Mark Daku, "On World AIDS Day, why the politics of AIDS is so important," *Washington Post*, December 1, 2018. https://www.washingtonpost.com/news/monkey-cage/wp/2018/12/01/on-world-aids-day-why-the-politics-of-aids-is-so-important/?utm_term=.6005597d3066.

Casey Quackenbush, "The Impact of President Trump's 'Global Gag Rule' on Women's Health is Becoming Clear," *Time*, February 4, 2018. http://time.com/5115887/donald-trump-global-gag-rule-women/.

Regina Boyle Wheeler, "10 Ways Motherhood Affects Women's Health," Everyday Health, December 14, 2012. https://www.everydayhealth.com/womens-health/ways-motherhood-affects-womens-health-3836.aspx.

For Further Discussion

Chapter 1

1. Why did Jo Baxter choose to have an abortion, even though she remained with her partner and they eventually married and had a child five years later? Did they make the right decision? Why or why not?
2. Why did members of the Save the 8th campaign feel that the defeat was a "tragedy of historic proportions"?
3. In South Korea, what does the decline in the opinion that abortion is akin to murder mean for the country's abortion ban?

Chapter 2

1. What percentage of women does Planned Parenthood serve who come from low-income families?
2. What are red flags that women should know to determine if their partner is sabotaging their birth control?
3. Should breastfeeding women have to carry around copies of state laws about public breastfeeding? Why or why not?

Chapter 3

1. Why does the intentional providing of misinformation about family planning make pregnancy more dangerous for teen mothers?
2. What are the connections between religion and contraception in Egypt?
3. Should religious exemptions to state child abuse and neglect laws be repealed? Why or why not?

Chapter 4

1. How many countries provide six months or more paid maternity leave? Should these countries also provide paid paternity leave as well?
2. How much more likely are women to have HIV if they have experienced intimate partner violence?
3. How does teen pregnancy impact immigration status?

Organizations to Contact

The editors have compiled the following list of organizations concerned with the issues debated in this book. The descriptions are derived from materials provided by the organizations. All have publications or information available for interested readers. The list was compiled on the date of publication of the present volume; the information provided here may change. Be aware that many organizations take several weeks or longer to respond to inquiries, so allow as much time as possible.

American Academy of Pediatrics (AAP)
345 Park Blvd, Itasca, IL 60143
(800) 433-9016
csc@aap,org
www.app.org

The mission of the American Academy of Pediatrics is to attain optimal physical, mental, and social health and well-being for all infants, children, adolescents, and young adults. To accomplish this, the AAP supports the professional needs of its members.

Center for Health and Gender Equality (CHANGE)
1317 F Street NW, Suite 400
Washington, DC 20004
(202) 393-5930
change@genderhealth.org
www.generhealth.org

CHANGE promotes the universal sexual and reproductive health and rights of women and girls. CHANGE's mission is to ensure that that sexual and reproductive health and rights are reflected in all US foreign policy and programming.

Center for Reproductive Rights
199 Water Street, New York, NY 10038
(917) 637-3600
press@reprorights.org
www.reproductiverights.org

The Center for Reproductive Rights is the only global legal advocacy organization dedicated to reproductive rights with expertise in both US constitutional and international human rights law. Their groundbreaking cases before national courts, United Nations committees, and regional human rights bodies have expanded access to reproductive health care, including birth control, safe abortion, prenatal and obstetric care, and unbiased information.

Guttmacher Institute
1301 Connecticut Ave NW Suite 700, Washington, DC 20036
(202) 296-4012
media@guttmacher.org
www.guttmacher.org

The institute produces a wide range of resources on topics pertaining to sexual and reproductive health and publishes two peer-reviewed journals, *Perspectives on Sexual and Reproductive Health* and *International Perspectives on Sexual and Reproductive Health*, and the public policy journal *Guttmacher Policy Review*.

International Planned Parenthood Foundation
4 Newhams Row, London, SE1 3UZ United Kingdom
+44(0)20 7939 8200
media@ippf.org
www.ippf.org

In the early 1950s, a group of women and men started to campaign vociferously and visibly for women's rights to control their own fertility. Family planning as a human right challenged many social conventions. Campaigners faced great hostility to gain acceptance for things that we take for granted today. Some were imprisoned. But they emerged determined to work with different cultures, traditions, laws, and religious attitudes to improve the lives of women around the world. And so, at the Third International Conference on Planned Parenthood in 1952, eight national family planning associations founded the International Planned Parenthood Federation.

International Women's Health Coalition (IWHC)
333 Seventh Avenue, New York City, NY 10001
(212) 979-8500
info@iwhc.org
www.iwhc.org

IWHC advances the sexual and reproductive health and rights of women and young people, particularly adolescent girls, in Africa, Asia, Eastern Europe, Latin America, and the Middle East. IWHC furthers this agenda by supporting and strengthening leaders and organizations working at the community, national, regional, and global levels and by advocating for international and US policies, programs, and funding. IWHC builds bridges between local realities and international policy by connecting women and young people internationally with key decision-makers. In doing so, IWHC brings local voices to global debates and in turn makes global processes and policies more understandable and actionable at the local level.

Joint United Nations Programme on HIV/AIDS (UNAIDS)
20 Avenue Appia, CH-1211 Geneva 27, Switzerland
+41 22 791 36 66
aidsinfo@unaids.org
www.unaids.org

Since it started operations in 1996, UNAIDS has led and inspired global, regional, national and local leadership, innovation, and partnership to ultimately consign HIV to history. UNAIDS is a problem-solver. It places people living with HIV and people affected by the virus at the decision-making table and at the center of designing, delivering, and monitoring the AIDS response. It charts paths for countries and communities to get on the fast-track to ending AIDS and is a bold advocate for addressing the legal and policy barriers to the AIDS response.

National Center for Health Statistics (NCHS)
1600 Clifton Road, Atlanta, GA 30329
(800) 232-4636
info@cdc.gov
www.cdc.gov/hchs

The mission of the National Center for Health Statistics (NCHS) is to provide statistical information that will guide actions and policies to improve the health of the American people. As the nation's principal health statistics agency, NCHS leads the way with accurate, relevant, and timely data.

Population Action International
1300 19th Street NW Suite 200, Washington, DC 20036-1624
(202) 557-3400
info@pai.org
www.pai.org

This organization's mission is to promote universal access to reproductive health and reproductive rights through research, advocacy, and innovative partnerships. Achieving this will dramatically improve the health and autonomy of women, reduce poverty, and strengthen civil society.

Power To Decide
1776 Massachusetts Avenue NW, Suite 200, Washington, DC 20036
(202) 478-8500
info@powertodecide.org
www.powertodecide.org

This organization provides trusted, high-quality, accurate information—backed by research—on sexual health and contraceptive methods so young people can make informed decisions. Their work creates opportunities for young people to get informed, take control, and advocate for themselves—and make decisions about the life opportunities that lie ahead.

The United Nations
760 United Nations Plaza, New York City, NY 10017
(212) 963-8687
info@un.org
www.un.org

Because of the powers vested in its charter and its unique international character, the United Nations can take action on the issues confronting humanity in the twenty-first century, such as peace and security, climate change, sustainable development, human rights, disarmament, terrorism, humanitarian and health emergencies, sexual equality, governance, food production, and more.

World Policy Analysis Center
621 Charles E Young Drive S, 2213-LSB, Los Angeles, CA 90095
(310) 825-7322
world@ph.ucla.edu
www.worldpolicycenter.org

The World Policy Analysis Center engages in a rigorous research process to gather and transform legal and policy data into the quantifiable, accessible, user-friendly resources found on their website, including interactive maps, tables, and downloadable datasets. Through partnerships with organizations around the globe, the center aims to translate its global policy data into community- and country-level improvements.

Bibliography of Books

Nina Brochmann. *The Wonder Down Under: The Insider's Guide to the Anatomy, Biology, and Reality of the Vagina*. London, UK: Quercus Publishing, 2018.

Charles C. Camosy. *Beyond the Abortion Wars: A Way Forward for a New Generation*. Grand Rapids, MI: William B. Erdmans Publishing Company, 2015.

David S. Cohen. *Living in the Crosshairs: The Untold Stories of Anti-Abortion Terrorism*. Oxford, UK: Oxford University Press, 2015.

Jonathan Eig. *The Birth of the Pill: How Four Crusaders Reinvented Sex and Launched a Revolution*. New York, NY: W. W. Norton & Company, 2015.

Betsy Hartmann. *Reproductive Rights and Wrongs: The Global Politics of Population Control*. Chicago, IL: Haymarket Books, 2016.

Abby Norman. *Ask Me About My Uterus: A Quest to Make Doctors Believe in Women's Pain*. New York, NY: 2018.

Willie Parker. *Life's Work: A Moral Argument for Choice*. New York, NY: Atria Publishing Group, 2017.

Rebecca Todd Peters. *Trust Women: A Progressive Christian Argument for Reproductive Justice*. Boston, MA: Beacon Press, 2018.

Katha Pollitt. *Pro: Reclaiming Abortion Rights*. London, UK: Picador Publishing: 2015.

Karen Weingarten. *Abortion in the American Imagination: Before Life and Choice, 1880-1940*. Rutgers, NJ: Rutgers University Press, 2014.

Vicki Oransky Wittenstein. *Reproductive Rights: Who Decides?* Minneapolis, MN: Twenty-First Century Books, 2016.

Index

A

acquired immunodeficiency syndrome (AIDS), 129–138

Advocates for Youth, 145–148, 150–53

Afghanistan, 90, 93

Africa, high rate of AIDS and HIV in, 129–138

Alito, Samuel, 52, 55

American Academy of Pediatrics, 102–106, 108–110

American College of Obstetrics and Gynecologists (ACOG), 77, 78, 80

American Thinker, 72–76

Amiri, Brigitte, 53

Andersson, Bjorn, 159–162

Antommaria, Armand H. Matheny, 102–106, 108–110

Argentina, 37

Avert.org, 129–138

Azmat, Syed Khurram, 90–96, 98–101

B

Bangladesh, 90, 93

Bargo, Michael, Jr., 72–76

Baxter, Jo, 25–29

Bloomstein, Lauren, 62–65, 67–71

Brazil, 37

breastfeeding, laws promoting, 142–143

Bridges, Emily, 145–148, 150–153

Brown, Rebecca, 139–144

Burwell v. Hobby Lobby Stores, 50–55

C

Calderón, Verónica Osorio, 35–39

California State Law AB 775 (Reproductive FACT Act), 85–89

Carey, Mary Agnes, 50–52, 54–55

Child Abuse Prevention and Treatment Act of 1974 (CAPTA), 106, 107, 111, 114

Chile, 38

China, restrictive abortion laws in, 44–45

Christian Scientists, 104, 107, 108

Clinton, Hillary, 28

Country Report on Human Rights Practices (CRHRP), 28

D

Deahl, Jessica, 123–128
Decoster, Kristof, 35–39
dilation and curettage (D&C), 27

E

Eaton, Sam, 97
Egypt, 90, 93, 94, 98
Eighth Amendment (Constitution of Ireland), 15, 30–34
El Salvador, 35, 37
Evans, Dayna, 56–61

F

Family Planning NSW, 154–158
First Amendment (US Constitution), 86, 87–88, 89, 117, 119
Followers of Christ, 16, 107, 111–119
Fox, Savanna, 19–24
France, more permissive abortion laws in, 139–144
Futures Without Violence, 79, 80

G

Global Gag Rule, 15, 38–39
Global Poverty Project, 30–34
Gorusch, Neil, 53
Guardian, 44–45, 111–119

H

Halappanavar, Savita, 31
Hebron, Tiernan, 28
Henry J. Kaiser Family Foundation, 50–52, 54–55, 149
Hitchings-Hales, James, 30–34
Hobby Lobby, 50–52, 54–55
human immunodeficiency virus (HIV), 129–138, 151
Hyde Amendment, 22

I

Idaho, 16, 111–119
Indonesia, 90, 93, 99
International Health Policies, 35–39
Iran, 90, 93, 94, 98
Ireland, 15, 30–34
Islamic countries, family planning programs in, 90–101

J

Jane's Due Process, 19–24
Jehovah's Witnesses, 105
Jordan, 90, 93, 95

K

Kasulis, Kelly, 40–46
Kuo, Lily, 44–45
Kuwait, 90, 93, 95

L

lactational amenorrhoea
method (LAM), 155–156
lady health workers (LHWs),
91, 93
Latin America, overview of
restrictive abortion laws
in, 15, 35–39
Little Sisters of the Poor, 53
lochia, 155

M

Malawi, 97, 130, 132, 134, 135,
136
Malaysia, 90, 93
Martin, Nina, 62–65, 67–71
maternal mortality, high rate
of in United States, 16,
62–71
Mazhar, Arslan, 90–96, 98–
101
medical care, right to refusal
of based on religious
grounds, 102–110, 111–
119
men, lack of reproductive
rights for, 72–76
#MeToo, 40, 41

Mexico, 35, 37
Montagne, Renee, 62–65,
67–71
Morocco, 90, 93, 96
Ms., 28

N

National Institute of Family
and Life Advocates
(NIFLA), 85–89
National Public Radio, 62–65,
67–71, 123–128
New York, 77–81
Nigeria, 90, 93, 96
Nixon, Richard, 16, 111, 107,
113

P

paid parental leave, 123–128
Pakistan, 90, 91, 92, 93, 98, 99
Paraguay, 37
parental consent, as
requirement for minors to
get abortions, 21, 22
partial-birth abortion bans, 22
PassBlue, 139–144
Pew Research Center, 107
Pilkington, Ed, 142–143
Planned Parenthood, 22, 24,
56–61, 66
*Planned Parenthood of
Pennsylvania v. Casey*, 22
postpartum depression (post-
natal depression), 157–158

postpartum medical issues, 154–158
preeclampsia, 62, 69, 70–71
pregnancy crisis centers, 85–89
Public Radio International, 40–46, 97

R

Reagan, Ronald, 15
Real Equality Between Men and Women bill, 140
Religious Freedom Restoration Act, 50, 54
reproductive coercion, 77–81
Roe v. Wade, 14, 19–24, 25–29
Rovner, Julie, 149

S

Sanders, Linley, 85–89
Sandstrom, Aleksandra, 107
SDG1, 14, 151, 161, 162
Shaikh, Babar Tasneem, 90–96, 98–101
Solis, Marie, 25–29
South Korea, 15, 40–46
Stoeffel, Kat, 77–81

T

teen pregnancy, high rate of in United States, 15, 145–153
Texas, 19, 20, 21, 22, 23–24, 62, 66

Texas House Bill 2 (HB2), 23–24
Texas Senate Bill 8, 24
Thailand, 159–162
Turkey, 90, 93

U

United Nations Human Rights Commission, 35, 36
United Nations International Conference on Population and Development, 93
United Nations' Millennium Development Goals, 139, 141, 144
United Nations Population Fund (UNFPA), 28, 135, 151, 161
Uruguay, 38
US Family and Medical Leave Act, 127, 128

V

Vice, 25–29

W

waiting period, as requirement for abortion, 22, 23
Weisem, Kathryn L., 102–106, 108–110
Wilson, Jason, 111–119
World Economic Forum, 159–162